# "Don't tell me you've fallen for Alex!"

Joanna was too overwrought to protest, and a look that was half compassionate, half angry crossed Nick's face. It seemed so natural for him to pull her into the sheltering comfort of his arms.

"Oh, Anna," he sighed. "You couldn't have chosen anybody worse than Alex to fall in love with!" Nick was so different from his brother, Alex. Nick was kind, considerate...and his fiancée, Shirley, was a lucky girl, Joanna murmured aloud.

"Shirley might not think so if she could see you both now," Alex's voice boomed from the doorway, chilling as ice water. Nick and Joanna turned to face the man Joanna loved—but Joanna knew from the look on Alex's face that after tonight her love for him would never be returned.

D1177299

# Devil on Horseback

by

ELIZABETH GRAHAM

*Harlequin Books*

TORONTO • LONDON • NEW YORK • AMSTERDAM
SYDNEY • HAMBURG • PARIS • STOCKHOLM

Original hardcover edition published in 1979
by Mills & Boon Limited

ISBN 0-373-02320-0

Harlequin edition published March 1980

Printed in U.S.A.

# CHAPTER ONE

'EXCUSE me, aren't you—Thomas?'

Joanna turned from her contemplation of the fountain before Vancouver's Court House where droplets of water sparkled in the early spring sunshine, her subconscious already attuned to recognising someone from her old school. Nowhere else had she been addressed by her surname only.

The violet blue of her eyes took in the tall rangy figure topped with a cloud of violently red hair.

'Yes,' she responded, hesitating only slightly before venturing: 'And you're Harper, aren't you?'

Sherry eyes sparkling, the other girl acknowledged her identity, pointing ruefully to her flaming carrot top. 'You could hardly miss, could you, with this trademark? What are you doing these days?'

'Nothing very much,' Joanna admitted with a faintly wry smile. 'How about you?'

'I'm beginning to make something of myself at last. Look,' the redhead said impulsively, 'have you time for coffee and a chat? It's not often I run into anyone from Fernside.'

Joanna successfully, she hoped, concealed her aimlessness from the other girl and agreed to a quick coffee, and minutes later they were seated at a rear booth in one of Vancouver's abounding small coffee shops.

Eagerly the red-haired girl launched into an enthusiastic description of the business she had started a bare eighteen months before, an agency for temporary and permanent domestic staff.

'It's just beginning to take off the ground now,' she enthused to the suddenly envious Joanna. 'People are getting to know us, and that we send reliable people, so we have lots of repeat requests for staff for social occasions. You know,' she expanded, stirring cream into her coffee, 'women who normally cope with their own household, but need help when their husbands entertain for business purposes or whatever.'

'Sounds wonderful,' Joanna smiled faintly. 'Maybe I should enlist in your army of domestics.'

'*You?*' Harper leaned back aghast. 'What in the world would you want with a job of any kind, let alone domestic? Correct me if I'm wrong, but I thought your father was Thomas Industries?'

'He was—is,' Joanna confirmed, her fingers tightening round the handle of her cup. 'It's just that—well, I'd like to do something on my own for once.'

'But domestic work?'

Shrugging, Joanna attempted a note of humour. 'Why not? I've taken a six-week course in gourmet cookery, and can produce *bœuf bourguignonne* and *rouget soufflé au fenouil* with the best of them!'

'Mmm.' The other girl looked thoughtfully at her. 'Didn't I read in the paper recently that your father had remarried?'

Trying not to sound defensive, Joanna returned: 'Yes. In fact, he and Marie are away on their honeymoon right now—it's a combined holiday and business trip.'

'So you're the poor little rich stepdaughter, left alone to while away the hours until Daddy comes home?'

Disliking the assumption that she had been pushed aside in favour of a young and beautiful wife, Joanna replied stiffly, 'It was my own choice to stay behind. Both of them wanted me to go with them, but I ...'

As her voice faltered away to nothing, the other girl supplied smoothly and not without sympathy: 'But you didn't want to play gooseberry to the newlyweds? Well, that's understandable. What isn't so clear is why you feel the need to prove anything. After all, the daughter of James Thomas must have had her future all mapped out years ago. Introduction to the best social circles, a mild flirtation or two before settling down to marriage with an eminently suitable man—wealthy, of course.'

Harper's half mocking summation of her life's purpose flicked Joanna on a spot that was too raw for a near-stranger's inspection.

'You make me sound like a robot with no mind of my own,' she said coolly. 'As a matter of fact, I've been into quite a few things since leaving school. Social work, helping to run a boutique, and—and acting.'

'Acting?' Red brows pencilled to darkness rose curiously. 'I go to most of the theatrical productions in town, but I don't recall having seen you.'

'No ... well,' Joanna's dark lashes fell to arcs over her smooth-skinned cheeks, 'I didn't have many actual on-stage parts. Quite a few actors start behind stage, you know, doing humbler things until ... until they're ready for ...'

'Oh, I see.' The light amber eyes regarded Joanna with a trace of compassion before glancing down at her watch. 'Look, I have to get back to the office, Thom—good grief, I can't keep calling you Thomas, can I? What's your first name again?'

Joanna told her, her brief flare of irritation fading in the envious realisation that the other girl's life was as full of vital purpose as her own was empty.

'Liz.' The redhead got to her feet and smiled down at

Joanna. 'Let's get together some time, hmm? In fact,' she
scrabbled in her shoulder bag and produced a leather
notebook, 'I'm free tonight, and if you are too and would
like to risk life and limb by sampling my cooking, why
don't you come over to my place and have dinner?'

About to refuse, Joanna paused and bit her lip. The
penthouse suite she shared with her father—and, on
their return, would share with Marie, too—was beautifully appointed, but empty. A flashing vision of the solitary dinner she would eat in the elegant dining room,
prepared by her father's efficient cook and served by his
unobtrusive maid, shot across her inner mind and without thinking she said:

'Thanks. I'd like that.'

After Liz had handed her a business card with her
home address printed neatly in the lower left-hand corner and given her the time of seven-thirty, Joanna still sat
in the booth submerged in her own thoughts. She scarcely
noticed that the waitress refilled her coffee cup, and she
stirred sugar and cream into it automatically.

The unfamiliar gall of envy rising to her throat was
difficult to push down. Did Liz Harper know how lucky
she was to be involved in a business of her own, being
independent, a person in her own right? Sighing, Joanna
admitted to herself with her customary honesty that it
wasn't Liz's opportunity she envied, but the obvious
efficiency with which she tackled the enterprise.

Her own father would have indulged her desire to enter any field of business, but his practical sense of
economics would have made him ensure that efficient
people ran it, leaving his daughter as a figurehead. And a
figurehead wasn't what she wanted to be.

A wry smile curved the petite but full bow of her
mouth. Maybe her father was right at that. Practicality

had never been her strong point, as had been proved by her abysmal failure in each of the fields she had tried.

Social work had been a disaster for her type of personality. She had intended working for a time as assistant to a qualified social worker before going to university to undertake her own training, but after a year she had been forced to give it up. Partly because of her superior's gentle discouragement, but mostly because she realised herself that she was too emotionally involved to be of much practical help to people in need of advice and help.

Her failure in her job at the boutique, a classily expensive one, was due to her inability to push obviously unsuitable sales on to uncertain customers. If a garment, however high-priced, looked awful on a client, Joanna was incapable of telling them otherwise, much to the chagrin of the shop's owner.

'If they like something, Joanna,' he would storm, 'it's not our place to persuade them to buy elsewhere!'

His request for the discontinuance of her services had been less politely expressed than the social worker's.

That brought her to her brief acting career. The Vancouver Shakespeare Players was a sophisticated group entirely devoted to the production of Shakespeare's dramas, and they had at first welcomed Joanna's petite and dark good looks, her hair a cascade of jet that would need no artificial aids to play time-honoured parts.

Unfortunately, Joanna's inability to remember more than six lines of dialogue at a time relegated her to tiny roles as a waiting woman or peasant in a crowd scene. And even that had proved a disaster when, in the course of coming to the aid of a young and nervous stagehand, she had missed her cue to speak the few vital words essential to the scene being enacted on stage.

Coming back to the present, Joanna realised that the

coffee she was still stirring in desultory fashion was stone
cold. Rising, she slid her arms into the heather blue
tweed coat she had discarded and made her way home,
remembering on her way out that Liz Harper had paid
the bill for their coffee.

Liz's apartment was on the top floor of a vintage house
not far from the city centre and Joanna, glancing round
after her arrival, liked its casual yet tasteful decor. Low-
slung couches blended with rattan cushioned chairs, and
a focal point in the small living room was what looked
like a buffalo skin stretched on a frame and hung from
the widest wall.

'I love it,' she enthused when Liz, clad in comfortable
multi-coloured caftan, brought her a rum punch from the
tiny dining room leading off the living room. 'It's cosy,
but interesting.'

'That's what I thought,' Liz returned with a grimace,
seating herself cross-legged on a floor cushion with her
drink, 'until my big brother came to inspect. To him, it's
a combination Oriental den of iniquity and a crash pad
for drug addicts!'

'Your brother,' Joanna frowned thoughtfully. 'Didn't
he come to the school gymkhana once?'

'You remember him!' chuckled Liz, settling herself
more firmly on her thick cushion. 'Once seen never forgotten. He's quite cynical now about the palpitation he
arouses in females from the age of sixteen to sixty!'

Sixteen ... Joanna had been sixteen that time when,
carrying the honours for her year at school, she had ridden Blueboy, taking him easily over the hurdles to a
clear win. Strangely, it was only now, sitting in his
younger sister's apartment in Vancouver, that she remembered the distinctively tall man in wide-brimmed hat

curled at the edges who had stood just behind the judge as he awarded Joanna first prize.

There had been approbation, even some admiration, in the smiling eyes shaded by the rancher's hat, and Joanna recalled in humorous self-deprecation her own young dreams woven around the man for the space of a week or two. Puppy dreams for an unattainable older man.

'Were your parents there that day?' she asked belatedly, still caught up in her early visions of masculine perfection in the form of Liz's brother, tall of limb and broad of shoulder.

'Our parents had died a couple of months before in an accident,' Liz returned tersely. 'Alex, as new head of the family, fulfilled his obligations to the letter, even to the point of attending his young sister's school occasions.'

'I'm sorry.' Joanna's sympathy was more than perfunctory. Hadn't she lost her own mother when she was only ten years old? 'Your brother must have been very young to take on such responsibilities at that early age.'

'He was twenty-four,' Liz acknowledged, looking up to smile briefly at Joanna. 'And I guess that was a bit young to take on not only three younger siblings, but a sizeable ranch as well.'

'Three?'

'My brothers Nick and Glen. Alex had been planning to marry Paula Erikson—her father ranches near us— but either he gave her the heave-ho or, as is more likely, she gave it to him when he became responsible for the rest of us. Paula isn't the kind to put up happily with a ready-made family,' Liz ended on a bitter note.

Trying to inject a touch of lightness, Joanna remarked: 'Well, it's just as well he found out sooner than later that his idol had feet of clay.'

'Hmm,' Liz returned gloomily. 'From what I hear, Alex hasn't learned one darned thing. In fact, he's building a fabulous new house at the ranch, and anyone with half an eye would know that it's for himself and Paula. She likes everything ultra-modern, and this house is that to its unfinished rafters.'

Joanna inserted gently: 'But if it's what he wants——?'

'Men always seem to want the worst possible things for themselves,' the other girl burst out, then threw back the remainder of her drink and rose lithely from her cushion. 'I'd better check on dinner.'

The goulash, accompanied by warm yeasty rolls, was superb and Joanna congratulated her hostess.

'This isn't something I could do,' she said with a wistful air, 'it's really delicious.'

'Well, it's far from *bœuf bourguignonne*,' Liz returned drily, 'which you can make and I can't! I can cope with plain everyday fare, which I was brought up on, but I'm pretty hopeless at gourmet dishes.'

'But they're really quite easy to do,' Joanna began eagerly. 'It might take a little more time than ordinary cooking, but the results are definitely worth it.'

'It's obvious you weren't brought up on a ranch!' Liz mocked as she rose and collected their empty plates. 'Everything has to be——'

Her wry observation was interrupted by the ringing of the telephone, imperative in its nearness on a nearby rattan-shelved stand. Excusing herself, Liz dropped the plates and went to pick up the receiver.

'Phil? I thought I told you—oh! Alex!' Seeming flustered suddenly, the red-haired girl shifted the receiver from one ear to the other. 'Yes, everything's fine here, but—what? Phil? He's just a friend of mine ... No, I'm too busy right now to hear the ring of wedding

bells, brother dear ... Good? What do you mean, good?
... You want me to *what*? ...' Liz's eyes had widened
over the receiver she clutched in her hand, but her jaw
clamped down suddenly as she listened to the voice at
the other end of the line.

'Alex, I *can't*!' she almost wailed. 'I'm just beginning
to get somewhere ... No, there's no way I can leave the
city now ... well, you'll just have to manage, won't you?
... I know it's my family, but ... oh, all right, I'll find
somebody, that's my business after all, isn't it? ... Yes,
yes, I'll call you as soon as I've found someone suitable ...' Her eyes swivelled round then to fasten thoughtfully on Joanna, who tried to look invisible. 'I have somebody in mind right now, Alex ... yes, she'd be perfect
... she's a wonderful cook ... Goodbye, Alex, I'll call
you as soon as I can.'

Joanna eyed the other girl warily as she came back to
the table, an air of suppressed agitation about her.

'Liz, I hope you're not——'

'Why not, Joanna? You said you were looking for a
job in the domestic line—what could be more opportune
than this? The housekeeper at home has been taken ill
suddenly and needs an operation. Alex needs somebody
to run the house and——'

'Run the house?' Joanna interrupted in amazement.
'Liz, I don't know anything about running an ordinary
house, let alone a ranch type one in the back of beyond!
How could I?'

'That's not important,' Liz told her tersely. 'Alex will
be content as long as there's a member of the female sex
inhabiting the nether regions of the house. The thing is,
Joanna,' she appealed, the sparkle temporarily gone from
her light brown eyes, 'there's no way I can leave my business right now. I'm just beginning to make a reliable

name for myself, and I have to be here to see that things run smoothly. Alex doesn't understand this—he's the old-fashioned type who thinks a girl's place is in the family home until she marries.'

Rising to her feet again, she added bitterly: 'And he can't understand that I'd never be interested in the kind of man I'd find around there. I have to prove to myself —and to Alex—that I can make it on my own.'

This Joanna could sympathise with, although she felt a sense of shock that Liz, despite all she seemed to have going for her, was really no better off than herself. Both needed to prove themselves worthy in their own right. Nevertheless ...

'Liz, there's just no way——' she began in a murmur, only to be interrupted by the other girl's impatient movement of her hand.

'It's not only that, Joanna,' she said urgently, seeming not to notice that she had sunk into her chair opposite Joanna again, 'it's that—well, you heard me mention Phil?' A soft glow lit Liz's expressive eyes, a tenderness Joanna couldn't ignore. 'He's very special to me, and I —well, I just don't want to leave him right now.'

'Surely if he feels the same way about you, a temporary parting won't make any difference?'

Liz drew down her mouth in a disparaging line. 'Normally, no. But Alex has a way of pulling people—especially men I'm interested in—down to less than their normal size. A couple of months at Clearwater Ranch could reduce Phil to pygmy size—in Alex's eyes, at least. And I couldn't bear that to happen again.'

The familiar protective instinct stirred in Joanna's breast as she looked across the table into Liz's distressed eyes. Evidently this older brother was autocratic in the extreme, caring little for his sister's happiness, if he had

broken up her previous romances. Determination flickered and grew in the deep recesses of her mind.

'Supposing I did agree to taking on this job,' she began cautiously, 'what would it entail?'

Liz's brow cleared, as if a weight had been lifted from
her. 'Nothing much really,' she said quickly. 'The men
are out most of the day, so it's just a question of flicking
a duster around in your own time, and throwing a meal
together at night. And a lot of the time there won't even
be that to do—Nick spends most of his free time with
Shirley, his fiancée, and Glen goes in to Williams Lake
to play the field of girls there.'

'And—Alex?'

Liz shrugged. 'He spends more time than anyone else
around home, but even he isn't there that much. Paula
Erikson sees to that.' Again there was a bitter note in her
voice, and Joanna looked at her thoughtfully.

'Surely if he marries this Paula, your problems will be
over permanently. Once she's there to take over the house
and meals.'

'Paula?' Liz crowed. 'I doubt if she's ever cooked a
meal in her life, and as for making beds and dusting ...'
The roll of her brown eyes was eloquent, and Joanna forgot her own ineptness in the household arts as she joined
in condemning the faraway Paula.

'She must realise that there'll be a certain amount of
that when she marries your brother. Even housekeepers
have a day off occasionally!'

'Paula will make sure she has lots of replacement
labour,' Liz returned drily, then went on more seriously:
'But that's in the future. Right now, Alex needs someone
to take care of the mundane details, and that person is
me if you won't take it on. I'll be honest with you,
Joanna,' she admitted frankly, 'not many people are an-

xious to take on such a job in the back of beyond, as you
called it. I've no trouble finding people to serve at a classy
cocktail party or take on more permanent duties in a
city household, but Clearwater is a proposition they don't
want to know about. A world inhabited mainly by horses
and cows hasn't much appeal to girls who want to see
boy-friends occasionally, or at least have the chance of
meeting prospective boy-friends.'

Joanna's sympathetic murmur brought Liz's eyes
quickly round on her.

'Is there someone you wouldn't want to leave for a
couple of months?'

'No,' Joanna replied slowly, 'there's no one special.'

Leonard Deline could hardly be classed as someone
special. He was an actor with the company she had
vainly tried to become a part of, and he was attractive in
a theatrical way, although Joanna had quickly seen
through his attentive pursuit of her, the daughter of
James Thomas. A struggling actor, however good-
looking, had the hungry look of someone in pursuit of
security in a monetary fashion. When the dust had
settled, they had emerged as good friends and saw each
other occasionally for dinner and a movie. Her relations
with other young men had been just as casual, with only
the rare exception.

'Will you do it for me, Joanna? It would save my life
in more ways than one, and——' Liz frowned. 'I'd forgotten about your parents. I guess they wouldn't be too
happy about you taking on a job like this.'

'At the moment, I don't think they'd care too much if
I took a job as a trapeze artist in a circus,' Joanna returned without rancour. 'Daddy's used to my harebrained
schemes by now, so I don't think I could ever surprise
him. Besides, they'll be away for at least another two

months, so they don't necessarily have to know about it until it's all over. If I take the job,' she added musingly.

'Please say you will,' Liz begged, her brown eyes large as she stared across the table at Joanna. 'I just have to have a chance to make this business go, prove to Alex that I can do something in my own right.'

Just as such a job could mean proving the same thing to herself, Joanna thought, but frowned as she returned Liz's stare.

'You're over twenty-one, as free as the birds. You make this brother of yours sound like an ogre from Grimm!'

'Oh, he's not,' Liz hastened to assure her. 'He's been a wonderful brother—look at the way he's cared for all of us all these years—but ... Well, he's just the tiniest bit old-fashioned in his ideas. You know the kind of thing— men are men and women are women and each has their place in the scheme of things. He put up the money to get me started, but I'm sure he thought he was pouring it down the drain.'

The two girls tossed the pros and cons back and forth while the first course was cleared away and the light dessert of canned peaches and cream disposed of, but Joanna was already feeling the tingle of anticipation at the thought of a new adventure. So what if her cooking skills were limited to a six-week gourmet cookery course? She had mastered that, and there couldn't be insuperable obstacles to producing lesser fare for the indiscriminate tastes of ranch men.

'There's just one other thing,' Liz said hesitantly when they sat down in the living room with their coffee. 'I think it's better if no one at Clearwater knows who you are. Alex particularly. I can't imagine he'd relish the thought of James Thomas's daughter serving his breakfast eggs.'

'You mean I'd have to change my name?' Joanna asked, startled.

'Not altogether. Thomas is a fairly common name ... how about if you become Anna Thomas? Just in case someone there might have seen something in a social column about you. You can be a poor but honest working girl with a family desperately in need of the money she slaves to procure.'

'You should be writing screenplays,' Joanna observed drily, 'not directing domestic labour. Suppose your esteemed brother doesn't fall for my act?'

'Isn't acting one of your accomplishments?' Liz asked in wide-eyed innocence. 'But make sure that Alex never finds out he's being deceived. He'll be a pet if he really believes you're what you say you are, but watch out if he ever finds out otherwise. He's formidable when he's angry.'

The slight quiver of alarm that rippled through Joanna went unnoticed by Liz as she went to the telephone to call her brother.

What had she let herself in for?

# CHAPTER TWO

RAIN cascaded from Joanna's sodden hair over her forehead and dropped from her nose to the drab grey of her raincoat. Rain hissed, too, from the night skies on to the pendulous branches of pines lining the broad highway and subsidiary road to its left. But Joanna had seen that landscape only from the brilliant lights of the bus that had dropped her at the crossroads leading to Clearwater Ranch.

The driver, disturbed in a fatherly way, said doubtfully as he took Joanna's luggage from the outside compartment: 'You're sure this is where you want to be?'

'Yes, I'm being picked up,' she had told him confidently, but now, an hour later, she knew that that confidence had been slightly misplaced.

The odd car that had passed did no more than throw up mud spatters on to her ruined hose, and her anger flared briefly as a massive truck slowed and the driver called suggestively: 'Want a ride, honey?'

Turning her back on the lumbering trailer, Joanna silently cursed Liz Harper and the autocratic brother who obviously felt no urgency about meeting the house servant his sister had engaged for him.

Her mutinously pursed mouth didn't relax, even when brilliant lights loomed up on the side road. The headlights of a husky jeep blinded her as it turned on to the main highway, picking up her drenched figure by the roadside. Too numb to look round, she hunched deeper into the upturned collar of her raincoat and heard the

19

U-turn the vehicle made before its engine roared up behind her and was reduced suddenly to a patient murmur
as the jeep halted beside her. A door slammed, then
there was the sound of heavy feet above the steadily hiss-
ing rain.

'Anna Thomas?'

The male depth of voice in the middle of this desolate
rain-soaked wilderness was reassuring, but Joanna let
her anger surface as she said icily:

'Is it likely there would be more than one stupid female
hanging around this godforsaken corner of the world on a
night like this?'

Her head turned to look at the looming figure beside
her, but she could see little of the man in the dim light
except for a quick assessment of bulk under a glistening
rain cape. His face was obscured by the pulled-down
brim of a wide hat which effectively warded off the rain
—a much more efficient item of clothing than the sodden
silk of her headscarf.

'I'm sorry I'm late,' came a clipped voice, 'but I'll explain about that on the way. You'd better get under
cover.'

It was on the tip of Joanna's tongue to make another
sarcastic remark, but she bit down on the words bubbling
to her lips. His tone of voice had already made it clear
that he would not expect smart remarks from a house
servant. And, heaven help her, that was what she had
agreed to be for the next couple of months.

A firm grip on her elbow propelled her into the front
passenger seat of the jeep, and the tall figure bent to pick
up her large-sized suitcase as if it weighed no more than
a hatbox. The suitcase, already showing signs of disinte-
gration, was a cheap one she had bought in the certainty
that no housekeeper would have owned the expensive

hide cases she normally used.

'I'm Alex Harper,' he informed her as he got behind the wheel—unnecessarily, Joanna thought sourly. Who else from Clearwater would have that arrogantly confident air?

She murmured something and relaxed into the warm cocoon of the jeep's interior. Never in her life had she felt so bedraggled, so miserably unattractive as she did at that moment. But the jeep was moving again, the hand that had been so firm under her elbow guiding the vehicle with equal confidence into the side road.

'How—how far is it to the ranch?' she enquired through teeth that were beginning to chatter as she thawed out.

'Only fifteen miles,' he answered, seeming preoccupied with the road ahead as he skilfully avoided most of the potholes gouged out by the rain. 'A bridge over the creek was washed out, that's why I was late. I had to rout out another couple of ranchers and between us we put together a crossing.'

'Oh!' was all Joanna found to say, ashamed of her previous anger at his evident lack of concern for her. It couldn't have been easy erecting a safe crossing over a rain-swollen creek, in the dark as well.

In deference to his enterprise, she subsided into the cushioned back of her seat. Was it her imagination, or was steam rising from her soaked hair?

She removed the dripping headscarf from the hair she had coiled into smooth neatness before her journey, and stretched out her sensible low-heeled shoes towards the low vent emitting hot air. Surreptitiously, she removed first one, then the other shoe, barely repressing a sigh of animal contentment as warmth enveloped her lower limbs. Her incarceration at Clearwater Ranch began to

take on again the spirit of adventure. Alex Harper in the
flesh might not be far from her previous conception of
autocratic ruler over a remote cattle empire, but he was
dependable, reliable, the kind of a man a girl could trust
to take care of her ...

Joanna was too uncomfortably wet to relax completely
into sleep, but her mind sank into a drowsy state until a
smothered oath from the man beside her jerked her into
wakefulness.

'What's wrong?' she asked as the jeep slowed to an impatient halt. A fuller glance sideways than she had given
him before revealed Alex Harper's set profile under the
dun-coloured hat. The dim outline of his face in the
dashlight showed strongly contoured features, a blurred
suggestion of thick eyebrows, an uncompromisingly
straight nose, and a firm jawline that was now clenched
to steely hardness.

'The bridge I helped resurrect seems to have disappeared,' he answered her question grimly, his eyes strain-
ing ahead through the wipers.

Joanna followed his line of vision to where the headlights illuminated the section of road immediately in
front of them, a rutted gravel strip which appeared to
end in a yawning chasm.

'Oh,' was all she said, but her midriff plunged in despair. 'What happens now? Do we spend the night here,
or what?'

She sensed the turning of his head, the sweep of his
eyes over bedraggled hair and face, and irrelevantly wondered what colour his eyes were.

'No, we don't spend the night here.' His tone spoke
volumes about her unattractiveness as a companion during the long hours until daylight made reconstruction of

the creek crossing feasible.

Joanna's feminine vanity was piqued for a moment until she reflected wryly that of course the mighty Alex Harper wouldn't dream of sharing the intimate confines of his jeep with the girl he had engaged as his cook-housekeeper. And certainly she looked the part of the downtrodden servant at this moment. But somehow, although Liz Harper would have been pleased at the initial success of their deception, the thought gave her little comfort.

'So what do we do?' she asked tartly. 'Swim across?'

'No,' he said again. 'We walk.'

'Walk?' she repeated stupidly.

'I'll check to see how high the creek's running,' he said, ignoring her question and pulling his hat further down on his forehead as he opened the door and went out into the driving rain.

Joanna saw his bulky figure retreat towards the chasm, leaning forward anxiously when, after a brief pause at the edge, he disappeared feet first down into the darkness.

Was he going to leave her there, alone in the dimly lit jeep? Or—what was even more horrifying—did he expect her to follow him down into the riverbed and pit herself against a raging torrent? Panicking, Joanna fumbled at the door catch and staggered from the vehicle, not noticing the headscarf that fell to the floor.

Rain lashed her hair and face, but she was beyond caring about that. She was in the middle of nowhere with a man she scarcely knew, yet he seemed the last human contact in a godforsaken world. Slithering on the muddy road, she reached the ridge by the river at the same time as he breasted the rise coming back.

'Why didn't you stay in the jeep?' he raised his voice to say irritably as he came to stand beside her. Then his head swivelled back to where he had climbed from. 'Still, you're going to get pretty wet crossing that. It's risen a foot or more in the last hour.'

He had raised his voice over the sound of raging waters below them, and Joanna peered sightlessly into the darkness. He must have cat's eyes, she thought edgily, to be able to see how much the boiling mass had risen. Her lips moved, and she took a hasty step back from the edge.

'What?'

She raised her voice and faced him in the car's headlights. 'I said I can't go down there ... walk across that —that ...'

She could have sworn that a smile tugged at the corners of his shadowed mouth, but his tone was matter-of-fact when he said: 'It shouldn't come much above your waist, I reckon.'

'My——?' A bubbling wave of hysteria washed over Joanna. It was a fine time to discover that Liz Harper's eldest brother was totally and completely mad! That thought sobered her, and she gathered her five foot three inches together and commanded him icily: 'Turn that jeep around and take me to the nearest civilisation. I'll pay you for your trouble in coming this far to meet me.'

'Thank you, ma'am,' he raised a bronzed wet hand to tip the edge of his hat, and this time there was definitely a smile on his well-shaped mouth ....a sarcastic grin. 'But as I'm in dire need of a housekeeper, and that's the job you've been hired to do, I've no intention of backtracking over miles of potholes just because you're afraid of a little water.'

'A *little*——?' she choked, gazing down again into the black void. 'Nothing on earth would persuade me to go down there,' she quavered, real fear in her voice as she turned sharply away and began to walk towards the headlights of the jeep.

'Except me, perhaps.'

Too fast for her to realise what was happening, she found herself spun round and lifted easily into strong arms. In another moment, Alex Harper had started on the slippery downward track to the increasing roar of the water.

'Put me down!' Joanna screamed, thrashing her legs uselessly and pummelling his chest with her fist.

'Stop that!' he commanded sharply. 'If you have to do something with your arm, put it round my neck!'

'I will not!'

His booted foot slipped as it entered the water, and Joanna needed no further encouragement to throw her arm round his neck, the other clamped firmly between his body and hers. She clung for dear life to the solid strength of him.

As he edged his way across, her eyes became accustomed to the darkness and her terrified eyes looked down at white foam as the creek gushed and broke over obscured rocks. She sensed rather than saw the sudden rise of water towards the middle and knew that it reached higher than Alex Harper's knees as he felt his way across the rocky creek bed.

Once more his foot slipped and he swayed precariously, steely arms tightening round her, Joanna moaned and buried her face in his neck, which was surprisingly dry under the shelter of his hat. Her grip tightened to a stranglehold, and she gave herself up to muttered prayers. So absorbed was she in her terror that she failed to notice they had left the water and were climbing the opposite bank.

His voice sounded loud when his head bent to her ear.

'You can let go now, you're safe.'

But it wasn't until he had set her on her feet and steadied her that her face lifted from the shelter of his neck. The jeep lights beamed from across the gap, amazingly close. It had felt like twenty miles from bank to bank.

Joanna clutched his arm as he turned away. 'Where are you going?'

His head swivelled back to her. 'To get the jeep,' he said with a tinge of impatience. 'I can't leave it there with the lights blazing, and I have to drag a couple of logs across the road to stop other traffic.'

'You're going back through that?' she asked disbelievingly through chattering teeth. 'You're crazy!'

'Would you prefer a ten-mile walk in the dark?' he asked drily, then: 'Stand well back and to the side when you see the jeep lights begin to move.'

Her mouth dropped open unattractively as she stared up at his shadowed face. 'You can't mean you're going to try to—to *drive* it over?'

'Exactly right,' he drawled. 'If you fear for my safety, you might try saying a few more prayers.'

With that he was gone, and time seemed endless until she saw his tall figure loom up at the far side. He lifted his hand in a wave and disappeared again behind the jeep. The rain had stopped, but the night was as dark as ever outside the perimeter of the headlights.

Another age went by, and then suddenly there was the slam of a door and a minute later the jeep began to move. Mesmerised, Joanna watched as it poised at the edge of the slope, then plunged suddenly, its lights illuminating the frothing water in terrifying detail before it splashed in with a shudder. Half way across the engine stalled, but roared back into life immediately and came powerfully through the water towards her.

It was only then that she remembered his injunction to stand aside, and she slithered back and to the side just in time. The engine strained up the slope and the jeep shot over the top, blinding her as the lightbeams flashed across her eyes.

'You *are* a crazy man,' she said unsteadily as he came towards her, but he seemed to hear that there was more of admiration than censure in her tone. His teeth flashed in a smile as he held her arm and piloted her to the jeep.

'Get in and get warm. I won't be long.'

'What now?' she sighed resignedly, shivering as the inside heat hit her. For a strange moment she felt she had known this brawny ranch man for a long, long time.

'I have to block off the road at this side, too,' he informed her without too much impatience, and disappeared again.

Joanna drowsed in the warmth until the driver's door opened and he slid behind the wheel. No shivering for him when the warm air surrounded him, she reflected curiously as he put the jeep in gear and moved off. A rancher's life must be a tough one, leaving no room for softness or indecision. None of the men she knew in the city would have dreamed of tackling a raging torrent like the one they were rapidly leaving behind ... but Alex Harper had treated it like an everyday occurrence.

The hands outlined against the wheel were long yet broad and bluntly competent as he guided the car once more over the muddied gravel road, avoiding the worst of the potholes, silent in his concentration. Hands a woman could trust with her life ...

Joanna jerked to a more upright position and was glad of the darkness that hid the rush of colour to her cheeks.

Where had *that* little thought come from?

From a tired mind and exhausted body, she told herself tartly, and gazed at the endless lines of pines edging the road at either side. Neither of them spoke for the space of fifteen or twenty minutes, then Alex Harper made a laconic comment as he turned on the gravel on to a smaller side road.

'This is Clearwater. The house is just another half mile now.'

'Li—your sister says you have a big place.'

'It stretches a few miles,' he admitted casually, the understatement of the year, she was later to discover. He turned his head to glance at her, the road smoother now.

'You know my sister well?'

'Er—no,' she said, not looking at him. She spoke the truth, but it felt like a lie on her lips. 'Really just—when she gave me the job here.'

'You're a little young to tackle a job like this.'

'Your sister told me it wouldn't be—too difficult.'

He gave a mirthless laugh and said with feeling: 'I'll bet she did! She'll say anything as long as it means she doesn't have to come herself.'

About to hotly defend Liz's right to independence, Joanna closed her mouth when he turned into a shorter driveway and followed a horseshoe curve up to the steps of a big, rambling—and darkened—house. Like a Colonial mansion she had visited once in Baton Rouge, the two-storied house was elaborately decorated with full-length balconies and wide porches. It looked eerie as it towered above them, and Joanna shivered.

'Come on,' Alex Harper said briskly, 'you need a hot bath and a change of clothes.'

Leaving the headlights on, he eased from behind the wheel and came round to open the door behind hers, extracting her suitcase from the rear seat, then pausing for a thoughtful moment before opening her door. 'We don't stand on ceremony here,' he said pointedly, and Joanna's slim back stiffened.

'Nor manners, it seems!' she said acidly as she swept past him up the wide white steps to the porch, biting her lip as she waited for him to follow her, which he did after another pause.

She wasn't playing her part of humble servant very well. Tomorrow, after a good night's rest, she would be better able to cope with Alex Harper and his arrogance.

He opened one half of the wide double doors, and she sensed a hint of sarcasm in the sweep of his hand which indicated that she should precede him. He bumped into her back when she halted suddenly just inside the doorway.

'Don't you have lights here?' she asked, panicking.

'We're fresh out of oil lamps,' he returned drily, 'but if you'll take just one more step forward, I'll see what I can do.'

Joanna heard her suitcase drop to the floor, and felt his body brush hers as he leaned sideways. There was a click, and she blinked dazedly round an immense hall. The light blinding her came from a huge chandelier suspended from the high ceiling, but after a moment her eyes became accustomed to its brilliance and she caught glimpses of a panelled oak staircase running up one wall, a long centre table with an elaborate centrepiece, a huge fireplace which looked as if it would take whole trees. Apart from a fur hearthrug and a couple of scatter mats, the floor was tiled in big red and grey squares.

'Well?' He looked at her expectantly and she blinked, not knowing just what it was he expected.

'It—it's beautiful,' she offered, and knew it was the

wrong thing to say as he frowned.

'Thanks. But do you think you'll be able to keep it in good order as well as coping with the rest of the house and the cooking?'

'Oh! Yes ... I'm sure I can.'

She shivered again as he propelled her by the arm across the tiles to the rear of the hall. Her tired brain acknowledged the necessity for an easily cleaned floor when her shoes squelched wetly as she walked.

'I'll show you the kitchen before you go and take your bath.' Turning lights on as he went, Alex Harper pushed open a door into a small rear hall with a passage running off to its left. Through another door straight ahead was the kitchen, big and square and with windows running along the entire length of a wall housing double sinks and adjoining counter tops. A large old-fashioned scrubbed wood table stood at the centre of the room, but gleaming appliances in a shade of avocado green abounded. The same green that graced the kitchen of the penthouse apartment she called home.

This time he seemed to expect no comment from her, and he led her at once along the passage outside the kitchen, stopping at the first of two doors and throwing it open. His hand reached for a switch and the room sprang into rosy light.

With a tight smile, he pointed out: 'The double bed is for the occasions when we have a married couple working in the house,' and Joanna's head came up with a snap.

'Really? I thought it was a gentle hint that I could entertain gentlemen callers—on occasion!'

His eyes narrowed, but he seemed unperturbed as he turned away to the door. 'You'll find ardour cools out here where a gent has to spend a considerable time reach-

ing his ladylove!' His head swung back from the door.
'You can hang your coat in the boot room opposite. It's
kept heated, so things dry pretty fast. Oh, and the bathroom's one door down. I suggest you take your bath,
then come out to the kitchen. I'll put some coffee on.'

He closed the door behind him, and Joanna heard him
cross the passage to the bootroom he had mentioned.
There was first one clunk, then another, and she listened
for a moment or two, but heard no sound of his leaving.

She stood woodenly in the middle of the room, too
weary even to appraise the rest of what was to be hers for
the duration of her stay. Dully, she wished that she had
told him she would go right to bed after her bath. She
was in no mood to cope with an inquisitive employer tonight, and something told her Alex Harper would be just
that.

Brightening at the thought of a hot bath, she undid the
buttons of her raincoat and opened the door cautiously,
peeping across the hall to where another door stood ajar.

Pushing the door open, half expecting to see Alex
Harper there, she sighed her relief and went into the
small room which was lined with open rods from which
hung what seemed like dozens of men's coats and jackets.
Her own coat looked ludicrously tiny beside the wet one
that had just been put there.

She glanced round and found the reason for the two
thuds she had heard. A pair of high boots stood next to
a contraption which was obviously meant for easy re-
moval of boots singlehanded. The brown leather had
darkened from its dousing in creek water, and she won-
dererd if its polish would ever return. That Alex Harper
would keep his boots in immaculate order was something
she knew instinctively.

*

Joanna's rightness was proved the moment she stepped into the kitchen. She had a brief opportunity to study Alex Harper as he stood with his back to her and lifted a coffee pot from the stove.

His brown check shirt was as freshly crisp as if it had just come from the ironing board and his slacks, though casual, were pressed to knife-edged neatness. Yet there was nothing effeminate about his sartorial perfection; not with that width of shoulder, or the muscled thighs under brown cord slacks.

He turned, two steaming mugs in his hands, and jerked his head back when his eyes lit on her in the doorway. Joanna was surprised to see that his hair was not the flame of Liz's, but a dark reddish-brown brushed thickly back from his face.

The coffee cups landed with a clatter as he stared across at her. For a moment it was as if he recognised her from somewhere ... somehow. She swallowed and came towards the table.

'Good God!' he exclaimed, stunned.

'Wh-what's wrong?'

Alex shook his head as his eyes went over the jeans she had pulled on after her bath, the simple white blouse, the warm glow in her cheeks and the black contrast of her hair, which she had tied into a ponytail.

'You're even younger than I thought ... and much too young to have a quarter of the experience my sister says you have.' He sounded angry, but his frown was thoughtful as he gestured her into the chair opposite the one he pulled out at the table.

Joanna helped herself to sugar and cream and played for time by stirring her cup industriously.

'Now,' he said at last, ominously quiet, 'put that spoon down before you wear out the mug, and tell me just what my sister's cooking up this time—pardon the pun.'

In a low voice, Joanna said: 'She's not cooking anything up.' Her violet eyes, large from weariness, fastened on his. 'She—she was kind enough to recommend me for the job.'

'Why? Liz usually has an angle when she's "kind" to someone.'

'Because she—she knew I needed this job.'

'Why?' he repeated ruthlessly. 'Are you supporting your parents or something like that?' The mockery in his tone adequately spelled out his disbelief on that score. Joanna's eyes dropped to his shirt front. The skin under his open collar was just a shade or two lighter than the brown check in the shirt.

'S-something like that.'

'What does your father do?' he shot at her, his glance following the movement of her hand as it picked up the spoon and stirred again in her cup. She stared intently at the circling coffee.

'He—he's not working right now,' she murmured, crossing the fingers of her free hand under the table in the hopes that her father was sleeping peacefully in some European bed at that moment.

'What does he normally do?'

'F-factory—he works in factories.'

'I see. And he's been laid off.'

The last was a statement rather than a question, and Joanna said nothing. Once the lies—or rather, the half-truths, which they were—started coming, they seemed to build on themselves and grow out of control.

'Well, I'm not entirely satisfied that there isn't more to this than you say,' he went on, his eyes narrowing when she looked up to gauge his expression. 'Why come away out here, for instance, when there must have been jobs in the city you could take?'

'I don't have any—I don't have *much* experience,' she

added hastily in correction, looking away again from his searching gaze.

'And my sister told you there was no need for it, hmm? Just a flick of a duster here, an occasional meal tossed off there?'

Joanna's eyes widened in surprise at the correctness of his mocking appraisal. 'I—well, something like that,' she admitted miserably, wondering once more what madness had prompted her to fall in with Liz's scheme. 'I'm sorry, I'll leave tomorrow.'

'Oh no, you won't,' he drawled softly, then leaned forward across the table, catching and holding Joanna's blue-eyed gaze. 'I don't believe half the things you've been telling me, but in case the bit about your unemployed father is the truth, I'd feel like a snake in throwing you out. Whatever scheme you and my sister have hatched up—and I can make a good guess as to what it is, based on past experience with Liz—I'm going to make it my business to see that you stay here. Not only that,' his voice dropped a notch, 'when you leave, you'll be such a dream of perfection in the household arts that you'll be able to snare a husband—maybe even a rich one—without pretending to be something you're not!'

He missed the perplexed look in Joanna's eyes when he got up and carried their cups to the sink, spilling the cold coffee into it and refilling them from the pot.

'Let's see if we can drink them this time,' he said drily as he placed hers before her. Abruptly changing the subject, he asked: 'Are you hungry? You must be ... it's hours since you've eaten.'

Joanna shook her head negatively. 'No, I—I'm not hungry. I—had a meal at one of the rest stops on the bus.' She kept her head lowered as she spoke the first real lie of the evening, and was startled when he strode to the huge refrigerator and opened the lower section impatiently. In a moment he came back with a plate covered in plastic wrap. Through the clear covering, she saw two chicken legs and a large helping of tossed green salad and one of potato salad. Despite herself, her mouth watered.

'The woman who's been helping out until you arrived,' he said, a momentary twitch at the side of his mouth, 'usually left a snack for my youngest brother, Glen. Roving the countryside foraging for unsuspecting females is his chief hobby, and he works hard at it.' Under the tone of light amusement, Joanna detected a caustic note, but she was too hungry at that moment to enquire further.

'But won't he want it when he comes in? He'll expect it if——'

Unwrapping the plate, Alex set it before her. 'He won't be back tonight. The bridge is down, remember?'

'What makes you think he won't do the same as you and drive across the creek?' she tossed up at him in a vain effort to discompose him as he had her a few minutes before.

'Because he knows I'd break his head if he tried it,' he returned pleasantly, then went to a drawer under a counter and came back with knife and fork and placed them at either side of the plate. 'Eat,' he commanded and, no longer able to ignore the clamour of her stomach, Joanna did.

Alex sat across from her, relaxed but watchful as he sipped his coffee and watched her enjoyment of the meal. Strangely, although a few minutes previously she would have felt painfully awkward to have him watch her eat, shyness had fallen away from her. But she almost choked when he said suddenly:

'You have beautiful hands. I like to see a woman with well-kept nails.'

She blushed, whether from pleasure at the unexpected compliment or because she had nearly asphyxiated herself, she couldn't tell. Murmuring something that could have been thanks, she sought for a change of subject. 'What about your other brother—Nick, isn't it? He'll be coming home, won't he?'

'You're very well informed about the family,' he remarked, a faint glitter coming into his eyes. 'But I'm sorry to tell you that you won't be meeting Nick either tonight. He'll stay at his fiancée's home overnight because——'

'He has to cross the non-existent bridge too,' she finished for him resignedly. Then her eyes were suddenly alert with realisation.

'You mean—you and I are alone in the house?'

He seemed surprised at the note of near-panic in her voice, his thick brows lifting as he said: 'I wouldn't have thought the prospect would be that alarming, considering the circumstances.'

The meaningful look his eyes sent her covered her with confusion. Of course he wouldn't expect objections from the servant quarter if an occasion arose when he was alone in the house with his housekeeper!

'No ... no, of course not,' she denied quickly. 'That's why I'm here, isn't it?'

The look in his eyes changed to a faintly puzzled expression for a moment, then he said slowly: 'Yes, it is, isn't it?'

Joanna rose and collected her dishes, remembering when she reached the sink counter that from now on, Alex Harper's dishes were her responsibility too. But when she turned back to the table he had already come up behind her, his emptied mug in his hand.

'Don't bother about the dishes tonight,' he said, leaning round her to put the cup on the counter, so close that she felt the air of virile maleness about him. She blinked owlishly at him when he went on: 'I leave the house around six, but I won't be back for breakfast till seven or so.'

'S-seven?'

'Seven,' he confirmed gravely. 'We eat breakfast in here, and lunch on the odd days when we're here, and dinner in the dining room. Of course, when we have guests we eat all meals in the dining room.'

'Guests?' she queried stupidly.

'We have overnight and weekend guests occasionally,' he smiled drily, as if aware of her trepidation. 'I'll show you the rest of the house tomorrow after breakfast. And now, you look about ready for bed.'

'Yes,' she agreed faintly, looking up into his eyes in surprise when he put a finger under her chin and raised it to his slightly smiling face.

'In the looks department, anyway, you're a vast improvement on most of Liz's hopefuls.'

Joanna's softly full lower lip trembled slightly with tiredness, the dark smudges under her eyes matching their black lashes. 'That sounds like a compliment of the backhanded variety, Mr Harper.'

As if trying to read something in the deep blue of her eyes, he stared intently down into them, then his face relaxed.

'I told you, we don't stand on ceremony here. You'll call me Alex, and I'll call you—Anna.' The name, on his lips, sounded like a soft caress and Joanna blinked, breaking the intangible something that had stretched between them momentarily. Pulling her chin away from his fingers, she sidestepped him and walked towards the door.

'Then goodnight—Alex,' she said in a cool drawl.

'Don't forget, breakfast on the table at seven,' he reminded her enigmatically, and she favoured him with no more reply than a faintly sour backward glance.

In her room, she noted that although there was a key-hole lock in the door, there was no matching key. Then, shrugging lightly, she moved away and began her undressing. Whatever else he might be, she was sure Alex Harper was no night prowler into his housekeeper's room, despite the strong fingers on her chin ... a touch that had inexplicably set her to trembling, as if she were still the sixteen-year-old who had woven tremulous dreams around his barely glimpsed figure at a school horse event. Tremulous—and temporary dreams!

While she waited for sleep to claim her in the big and superbly comfortable bed, she pushed aside thoughts about her total inadequacy for the job she had undertaken, and concentrated drowsily on Alex. About the confident way he moved, the well-knit way his body had been formed, the healthy vitality of his russet hair.

And his eyes, which were the warmest shade of brown she had ever seen ...

# CHAPTER THREE

In her dream, she fought a losing battle of wills with a magnificent chestnut horse which bucked and reared and ignored her attempts to tame his independent spirit. As the animal's head twisted upward in her direction, the brown of his eyes glinted mockingly into hers, as if daring her to take him on in the final battle. *I'll always win,* those eyes said, and Joanna struggled desperately to throw off the incongruously lifted hoof that rocked her shoulder roughly.

'No! Stop it!' she commanded imperiously, then slid comfortably back into the yielding mattress and felt sleep claim her again as warmth from the high lofted quilt enfolded her.

The movement at her shoulder began again, with more force than before, and she rolled irritatedly away from its weight through the covers. 'Go away,' she moaned.

'Not until you're on your feet,' a grim male voice answered, and Joanna came instantly to wakefulness. Her breath drew in on a startled exclamation as she turned and shot upright in the bed.

Alex Harper's expression, as he glared down at her, was malevolently wide awake. His eyes, cool, not warm as she had remembered them, followed the movement of her small hand as it swe aside the long silken threads of black hair from her face. He looked disgustingly fresh, as if he had been up and about for hours.

She realised sluggishly that his eyes had dropped to the low-cut flame-coloured nightdress she was wearing, his

gaze deliberate on the gentle swell of her curves into the
lightly frothy material. Hastily, she drew the covers up
to her shoulders and gasped:

'You shouldn't be in here when I'm in bed!'

'And I shouldn't have to go out to a hard day's work
on an empty stomach,' he countered irritably, his eyes
lifting to go abrasively over her dishevelled hair and
cloudy violet eyes.

Remembrance rushed over Joanna and she asked
faintly: 'Wh-what time is it?'

'Long past the time when you should have been up
and busy in the kitchen,' was his abrupt rejoinder. 'Are
you going to rise under your own steam, or do I have to
dump you under a cold shower?' The grim fold of his
mouth revealed how much pleasure that idea gave him.

Joanna compressed her own mouth and gathered the
wisps of her dignity round her. 'Give me fifteen minutes
and I'll be on duty—*sir*!'

'Make it ten,' he returned silkily, 'and I'll consider
keeping you on as cook here.'

He spun away on one booted heel, his body held tautly
in beige twill shirt and close-fitting work trousers as he
marched to the door, catching Joanna's childish poking
out of her tongue at his retreating back.

Ignoring the infantile display, he went on curtly: 'Nick
and Glen will have eaten where they spent the night, so
you've no need to bother about them this morning.'

To the firmly closed door Joanna mouthed silently as
she threw back the covers and stepped into a chilly
morning. 'Oh, thank you for small mercies, my lord!
And did you sleep last night? Me? Oh, just beautifully
in this strange but comfortable bed, thank you for your
concern. Breakfast? Yes, *sir*, coming right up.'

Cold reality hit her ten minutes later when, within the specified time, she entered the well-equipped kitchen. What did a rancher eat for breakfast?

Eggs? Yes, definitely. Bacon? Another definite. What else? Toast—yes, he was certain to want that. Coffee. Its tantalising aroma was already making her nostrils twitch, and she crossed to the big percolator and reached for a mug hanging from a row of pegs beneath a bank of cupboards. Not bothering with sugar and cream, she sipped gratefully on the black brew, feeling life return to her sleep-sodden limbs. Her brain, too, was beginning to stir to alertness when the kitchen door opened and Alex stood on the threshold.

'Breakfast?' he reminded her with a grimly martyred air, and she reluctantly put down her mug and stepped towards the refrigerator.

'Right away. How do you like your eggs?' she asked, remembering countless enquiries from faceless waitresses over the years.

'Sunny side.'

Wishing he would not just stand there and watch her take eggs and thickly sliced bacon from the refrigerator, Joanna assumed an air of nonchalant ease as she un-hooked a small-sized frying pan from the array over the cooking area, and separated two of the substantial slices of bacon and placed them in the pan.

After an abortive effort to manipulate the stove, when a small rear burner glowed redly and left the larger coils under the pan greyly cold, Joanna breathed a silent sigh of relief when the bacon began to sizzle and sent out an appetising aroma.

The first egg broke and oozed yellow yolk over the rapidly congealing white, but the second was a perfect oval of pale yellow in thick white surrounds. She nursed this one and almost cried when, after she had scooped the bacon and badly battered first egg on to a plate hastily taken from the cupboard above, her prize succumbed to her too-enthusiastic manipulation of the scoop and spilled its yolk apologetically on to the white.

The master of Clearwater surveyed his breakfast distastefully as she placed it before him. At last he said, as if dredging up the words from deep inside him:

'Isn't something missing?'

Joanna gazed blankly down at the unappetising plate. 'Toast,' she muttered. 'I forgot the toast.'

Glad to retreat from his stricken male regard, she searched through the cupboards until she uncovered a toaster, and subsequently bread in a closed container above the counter. With almost feverish concentration she watched until the slices popped up, golden brown and glistening as she applied generous strokes of dark yellow butter.

'There!' she announced triumphantly as she placed the small plate at Alex's left hand. 'Would you like marmalade, or—whatever?' she gestured vaguely towards the cupboards.

'No,' he said faintly, gazing fixedly at the congealing eggs and half-cooked bacon before him. 'This is more than enough.'

Satisfied, Joanna retreated again to the coffee pot and poured herself another cup, this time adding cream and sugar from the dishes on the table. 'More coffee?' she asked brightly, observing that the large mug beside Alex stood empty.

'Please,' he requested bleakly, laying down his knife and fork with alacrity when she brought the refill to him and drinking deeply of its contents.

Dropping into the chair opposite, Joanna asked conversationally: 'Aren't you hungry?'

'No,' Alex returned heavily. 'No, I seem to have lost my appetite.'

'I'm not surprised,' she chuckled, lifting her coffee cup to her mouth. 'How anyone could face a cooked breakfast at this time of the day beats me.'

'Yes.' He looked down again at the scarcely touched mess of his breakfast. 'Me too.'

There was a faint rat-tat of heels over a tiled floor, then the kitchen door swung open.

Joanna's head swivelled and she observed a young man of a little more than medium height in the doorway. His light suede jacket was topped by eyes the shape and colour of Liz's, and hair several shades lighter, and brighter, than Alex Harper's.

'Oh. Hi.'

Sherry-coloured eyes swept between Alex and Joanna, lingering in startled appraisal on her black hair drawn back into a hasty ponytail, and on the small oval of her striking features of violet blue eyes and softly bowed mouth over firmly rounded chin.

Alex rose to his full height, a few inches above the other man's, and introduced them briefly. 'This is my brother Nick—Anna Thomas, our temporary housekeeper.'

Was there a note of relieved stress over the word 'temporary'? Joanna didn't take time to analyse it then as she rose to greet Alex's brother.

'Well, hello!' The light eyes roved over Joanna's trim appearance in white blouse and jeans, the clothes she had worn the night before and pulled on in her hurry that morning. Appreciative eyes that poured balm on her ruffled spirit.

'Would you like some coffee?' she offered, standing away from the table and going towards the pot on the stove.

'I sure would. Thanks—Anna.' The newcomer pulled out one of the side chairs at the table and sat down, his older brother following suit after a brief pause. 'How come you made it across the river last night? I'd have sworn that neither man nor beast could have crossed it.'

'I managed,' Alex said laconically. 'How does it look this morning?'

'Slim Bruder and Hank Benson must have been busy at first light,' Nick returned, then looked up to smile at Joanna as she placed a full cup of coffee before him. 'I guess you made it back just in time last night.'

'I guess,' his brother said noncommitally, rising again to his feet. 'When you've finished that, you'd better come on out. The rain's washed out a lot of the fences, and I don't want any of the stock roaming where they shouldn't. I'm heading up towards the north pasture. You can go south and work up to me—Glen, too, when he finally gets here.' There was a note of exasperation in his voice as he walked to the outer door, his boots grinding into the tiled floor. Turning back there, he added: 'I'm running late, Anna, so you'd better discover the rest of the house for yourself. I'll get the bunkhouse cook to set up some lunch, but we'll all be here for dinner at seven.'

So saying, he departed and left Joanna looking wistfully from the bank of windows behind her as his tall figure shrugged into a brown plaid jacket and stomped off across a dew-wet grassed area at the back, disappearing presently behind a belt of shelter trees separating house from ranch buildings. A sigh escaped her.

'Don't let Alex bother you,' Nick said quietly from

the table. 'His bark's an awful lot worse than his bite.'

'Is that a threat or a promise?' she quipped lightly as she came back to her cooled coffee and regarded him over the rim of her cup. 'Does he always eat such a small amount for breakfast?'

Nick's eyes fell on the plate his brother had left, noting the congealed bacon slices and barely touched eggs. 'No, he usually eats a good breakfast,' he said slowly, 'it's a long day out there sometimes. Still,' his brow cleared, 'at least he ate the steak.'

'S-steak?' Joanna's hands tightened on the cup. 'I never heard of anybody eating steak for breakfast!'

'You mean you didn't——?' Nick looked nonplussed, then said with awe: 'No wonder he was in such a bad mood! If there's one man who needs his protein, it's Alex.'

'There's protein in bacon, and there's protein in eggs,' Joanna snapped, suddenly tired of the discussion of Alex Harper's diet. 'If he'd craved it, he would have eaten what I prepared for him.'

'Mmm. I guess you're used to——'

Nick stopped talking when a distant clamour reached into the kitchen. An unmelodious male voice crooned one of the recent pop hits as boots rattled noisily over a tiled floor. Then the kitchen door was thrust open and Joanna stared in amazement at the young man framed in the doorway. His lanky figure, dressed in crumpled jeans and equally creased silk-like blue shirt, was topped by a face freckled and still boyishly rounded and a flame of carrot hair even brighter than Liz's.

'Wow! *You're* the new housekeeper?' he asked disbelievingly in a voice Joanna suspected was more subdued than normal. His eyes, the Harper brand of brown, flicked quickly over her and left her feeling as if there wasn't much of her anatomy he hadn't examined and assessed.

'This is my kid brother, Glen,' Nick introduced wryly. 'Miss Anna Thomas, Glen.'

'How do you do?' Joanna murmured, wondering at the spectrum of hair colour in the Harper family, from the reddish brown of Alex's to the blazing top of Glen's.

'How do *you* do?' Glen advanced into the room, tossing a blue denim jacket on to the chair he sat on like a butterfly alighting for a few moments only. 'If you cook as well as you look, you could be my ideal woman.'

'She hasn't been invented,' came a dry comment from the outer kitchen door, and three pairs of eyes swivelled in startled surprise to the deceptively indolent form of Alex Harper draped lazily against the doorframe. His voice sharpened as he looked at his younger brother. 'Where the hell have you been till this time of the day?' He made it sound as if the clock had leapt forward to two in the afternoon, instead of the barely eight-thirty it registered.

Glen's face took on an embarrassed redness, whether from the censure in his brother's voice or the fact that it had been offered in front of her, Joanna didn't know. But she bristled on his behalf.

'You know very well that the bridge was down,' she defended. 'You said yourself that you didn't want him to——'

'I was talking to my brother, Miss Thomas,' Alex intervened, his voice smooth steel and just as cold. The eyes, which could seem so warm and human on occasion, were trained unrelentingly on the youngest Harper. 'Well, where were you?'

Snubbed, Joanna subsided, but her heart went out to the boy, who flicked his tongue nervously over his lips as he looked up at Alex and away again.

'I—met this girl in town last night, and—when the storm got bad, she—she took me to her place.'

'Her family was there?'

'What do you think?'

'It's a question of facts, not what I think might have happened,' his brother bore down remorselessly.

'Her parents live up north,' Glen admitted sulkily at last. 'She has her own place in town.'

The middle brother spoke then, and Joanna immediately labelled him 'Nick the Peacemaker' because his quietly spoken words fell as a balm between the two extremes of brotherhood.

'He had to stay somewhere, Alex, with the bridge being down. As I see it, he didn't have much choice but to accept shelter where he could get it.'

'There are family friends like the Steeles, the Braders, the Harvards,' Alex retorted caustically, but his ire towards Glen seemed to have evaporated somewhat. 'Anyway, enough time has been wasted for one day. Let's get it moving.'

As his brothers shrugged into their jackets, he came further into the room and said quietly to Joanna: 'By the time I come back, I'll expect a gleaming house from attics to cellars—and a meal on the table at seven.'

'Yes, *sir*!' Joana was still smarting at his relentless interrogation of Glen's movements. His eyes narrowed on her challenging blue gaze.

'Don't censure me for my handling of Glen,' he warned softly, hearing as she did the departure of his brothers for the outdoors. 'He needs a firm hand at times ... but you wouldn't know about that.'

'What would a mere housekeeper know about human relationships?'

'Ranging from very little to quite a lot,' he said enigmatically, 'depending on her age and experience.'

Leaving the conversation at that level, he wheeled about and left the house again, tall and immovable in his beige workpants and blending plaid jacket. As Joanna watched from the window, a shaggy black-haired dog hurtled from the trees to greet him, prancing its delight as he bent to caress the half droop of silken ears.

A female, no doubt, Joanna thought sourly as she started to clear the table of its few dishes. She had come to the conclusion that only a female animal, unaffected by the human elements of social intercourse, could display such uninhibited pleasure in the company of a man she was beginning to regard as even more autocratic than Liz had led her to expect.


After looking doubtfully at a gleaming and frighteningly large dishwasher, Joanna dumped all the dishes in one of the steel-lined sinks and fled to the main part of the house. She would do an inspection of her own, uninhibited by Alex Harper's overweening presence.

The main hall seemed even larger than it had the night before, and she moved quickly across it and into a dining room through an archway to her right. A polished table, flanked by high-backed side chairs and two more elaborate chairs at either end, designed obviously for master and mistress of the house, was centred over Italian-styled vinyl flooring, complementing the vast elaboration of built-in polished wood buffet and plate-decorated hatch. A bank of windows along one wall, patio doors at its centre, gave out to the front veranda, and a similar lay-

out opened to the view of circular driveway and green
meadows in the living room across the hall.

The furnishings in that room, Joanna realised as she
glanced round it, were far less ostentatious than the furnishings of her father's luxurious apartment in Vancouver, but there was a homespun warmth in the floral
upholstery of sofas and chairs, the predominant rust of
giant flowers exactly matching the colour of wall-to-wall
carpeting. Another capacious rock fireplace dominated
the far wall, and books on shelves flanked the glistening
stones.

Up the wide staircase, with its small landing a few
steps up from the hall before branching sharply left to
the upper floor, Joanna trod softly, feeling a usurper of
privacy ... Alex Harper's privacy. The house seemed to
await his vital presence to bring it to life, to a purpose in
being.

Bedrooms and bathrooms opened off a central upper
hall, and Joanna had little difficulty in locating Nick's
room, with its portrait of a fluffily fair-haired girl with an
infectious smile on the table beside his bed, nor Glen's
room with all its paraphernalia of sports equipment, pen-
nants, prize cups and an inordinate number of scantily
clad voluptuous females pinned to the walls.

Smiling, Joanna progressed to a larger room where a
massive bed lay royally between two long windows over-
looking bright green lawns that stretched to fit the contours of a lazily winding silver river ... the clear water
described in the name given to the ranch?

The room, which was more like a luxurious suite, was
obviously the master bedroom, but a thoughtful glance
round told Joanna that Alex Harper didn't occupy it in
solitary state. His room must be one of the other two on
this upper level which she hadn't yet inspected and,

moved by curiosity to see the lair where Alex had his being, she left the master bedroom with a half wistful glance back at its solid furnishings ... evidently Alex intended using it only when he brought his wife to Clearwater.

And he had already chosen the wife who would share this master suite with him, she thought as she poked her head into first one and then the other of the remaining bedrooms without finding any evidence of his occupancy.

Puzzled, she retreated down the staircase and noticed a door across the hall to the right of the fireplace. As she opened it, her brows lifted in recognition of the pure masculinity the interior revealed. Black leather sofa and chairs were arranged round yet another fireplace and books lined two of the walls. A black leather-topped desk was angled before two high windows on the far wall, and on the right was another door.

Crossing the thick red carpet covering the floor, Joanna reached for the handle and knew as the door opened that she had found Alex's lair. A bed, not quite so massive as the one in the upstairs suite, dominated the good-sized bedroom, drawing attention with its tossed sheets and blankets. Joanna's lips tightened. Alex gave the impression of being a neat man, but the disarray in his bedroom said the opposite. Half open drawers spilled their contents as if impatient hands had raked through them, and the laundry hamper in the adjoining bathroom bulged over the top.

Joanna closed the door on the mess and went back to the kitchen, her mind already busy with thoughts of the dinner she would prepare that evening. This first dinner would be the one to make a lasting impression, and she wanted perfection.

A frown marred her darkly marked features as she

rifled through the kitchen cupboards and refrigerator. The ingredients for a mixed salad were there ... lettuce, celery, green onions and peppers, tomatoes ... but what should she serve for the meat portion of the meal? Not more of the bacon Alex had rejected at breakfast time ... but Nick had said that Alex loved his protein ... Cheese. Eggs. Both contained protein, and merged into a soufflé, would make a nourishing meal.

That decision made, she put on fresh coffee and made herself some toast for her delayed breakfast. Sitting alone at the kitchen table, she felt the loneliness surrounding her, the hum of the refrigerator the only sound breaking the profound silence. A quick glance round told her that there was no radio, and she berated herself for not bringing her own. Even a low-tuned murmur would have brought a breath of the outside world into the silent house that seemed to wait ... for what?

Sighing her impatience at her own fancies, Joanna rose and set off to become more intimately acquainted with the lower floor of the house—in particular, the red and grey tiles in the huge hall, which showed the imprint of muddy feet in a track from front door to kitchen quarters.

Armed with a long-handled sponge mop taken from a well-equipped storage cupboard next to the cloakroom, and a plastic bucket of hot soapy water, she returned to the hall and stared thoughtfully round at the vast expanse of floor. It would take hours to go into and under every nook and cranny. Giving a slight shrug of her shoulders, she marched decisively to the front door and, moving backwards from there, sponged only the tracked area.

In an access of energy, pleased at the ease with which the hall had been restored to gleaming brightness, she tackled the kitchen floor next. The mop made easy work of that too and, satisfied, she sipped on a cup of warmed-up coffee while surveying her handiwork.

This job wouldn't be as difficult as she had imagined. The house was big, but with a little ingenuity and organisation it should be easily manageable.

It was a lovely house, too, she reflected. The charm and warmth of a house long and well lived in was something she knew little about. She and her father had always lived in apartments since her mother's death, a series of apartments which had grown more and more luxurious with each move. And always there had been the unobtrusive ministerings of domestic staff to make it seem as if the household ran on oiled wheels.

Certainly Joanna, on her holidays from school and afterwards, had never been asked to contribute to that smooth running. Any offers of help were firmly turned down by the current domestic staff and James Thomas, absorbed in the business life he had immersed himself in after his wife's death, had been less than understanding of his daughter's need to be needed.

'Don't interfere, honey,' he had told her on numerous occasions. 'I pay them well for what they do, and they know I expect them to perform well. Why don't you go down to the stables tomorrow and do some riding?'

And that was what Joanna had done most days. Her father's limousine and driver had been available to her after his early morning trip to the offices of Thomas Industries, and she would spend hours each day riding and grooming her own chestnut mare at the boarding stables just outside the city. Small wonder that she had become the excellent horsewoman she was, silver cups and trophies taking the place of cherished dolls in her lavish bedroom.

Sighing again, she got up and wandered to the windows, cup in hand. Riding in this country must be fantastic, she thought wistfully, gazing out across the green lawns to the belt of trees dividing working area from house and beyond that to a wide expanse of rolling prairie land. But the Anna Thomas she was supposed to be, the daughter of a city factory worker, would hardly be expected to have proficiency in horseback riding.

After refilling her cup, she went back to the table and idly picked at her nails where the caustic soap from her floor washing had made the near colourless polish lift in places. Alex Harper had remarked that she had lovely hands, that he liked a woman with well-kept nails. The unexpectedly gallant compliment still staggered her, but suddenly the gentle smile curving her mouth disappeared and she sat up sharply.

She should have known that there was a hidden meaning behind a compliment from Alex Harper! Although he had sounded sincere, it was obvious to her now that he had simply been interrogating her in a different, more subtle way than he had employed before that.

What an idiot—a fatuous idiot!—she had been to think that a man like him would pay compliments to his housekeeper. Nothing a man of his type did or said could be taken lightly, there was always relentless purpose behind it.

She pursed her lips mutinously, then shrugged. So what if he suspected she wasn't what she said she was? Any real housekeeping Anna would have nails kept short and pratically unbreakable in deference to the practicality of her job. Well, if short nails were what he expected, that was exactly what he would get.

Ten minutes later she had filed the offending ovals

down to a point where they barely showed beyond the tips of her fingers. Holding them up to her own critical inspection, she gave a satisfied grunt. 'Let's see what you make of them, Mr Arrogant Harper!'

# CHAPTER FOUR

As it happened, Joanna was too busy and flustered to know or care about Alex's reaction to anything except the dinner she served to him and his brothers in the dining room at seven.

What had at one point seemed an interminably protracted afternoon telescoped with frightening suddenness into an awareness of time, of the imminent arrival of the Harpers for their first meal prepared by their untried housekeeper. Gone were the leisurely moments when she had laid the attractive oval dining room table with stiff white linen, heavy silver cutlery and exquisitely cut wine goblets from the side buffet.

The general mode of entry seemed to be through the back porch into the kitchen where first Glen, his eyes dancing in anticipation, sought and found her slender form bent over the sink preparing salad vegetables, then Nick with his soberly intent look. Last of all came Alex, his eyes reaching in more leisurely fashion across to Joanna's apron-clad figure.

His mocking glance went from the startled blue of her eyes to the clumsily tied white apron over slim blue sheath dress. As if it was her fault, she fumed silently, that the regular housekeeper had a much more ample girth than her own!

Glen, however, had no such reservations.

'Wow!' he exclaimed exuberantly, turning back to Nick with a grin. 'Pinch me to make sure I'm not dreaming all this. A girl who looks like fifty movie stars rolled into one preparing *our* dinner!'

'I'll do more than pinch you if you don't get moving,' Nick growled, yet his smile in Joanna's direction was sweet and friendly.

Alex lingered when his brothers had clattered noisily across the tiles to the boot room beyond the kitchen. A brief encompassing glance told Joanna that his clothes bore the evidence of a long rough day. He had removed his jacket on entering the house, and his sweat-stained beige denim shirt matched the creased pants that clung to his lean hips as if moulded there. His boots had a film of mud on them that obscured the high polish of morning.

'How is it going?' he asked in perfunctory fashion, as if his real thoughts were elsewhere.

'Fine,' she replied, equally short. 'I'll be serving dinner promptly at seven, so I hope you'll be ready then.'

With pointed dryness, he said: 'Don't worry. We're all more than anxious to sit down to a good meal by the time seven comes around.'

The firm tread of his boots receded from her as she concentrated on tossing the salad in a huge wooden bowl, then she directed her attention to the soufflé. But hardly had she begun the tedious grating of the cheese when Alex was back, soft-footed this time in moccasin-type slippers.

'Just where had you planned on eating your meal?' he demanded belligerently.

'In the kitchen, of course,' she returned absently, her breath drawing in on a pained hiss when the cheese slipped and she grated her fingers instead.

'You'll eat with us in the dining room. It's bad enough having to work with my brothers all day long without having just their company for the evening meal. Lay another place for yourself.'

'Yes, *sir*,' she snapped in irritation as the last of the cheese disintegrated into unmanageable blobs. 'Anything else, sir?'

'Yes, You can stop "sirring" me, and you can——' His voice broke off abruptly. 'What in hell have you done with your nails?'

Giving up on the cheese remnants, Joanna gave him a long-suffering look. 'My nails? Oh. Well,' she improvised lightly as she rinsed the grater under the tap, 'I can only grow them in between jobs, you know. Housework and groomed fingernails don't go together.'

'Haven't you ever heard of rubber gloves?'

'I don't like them,' she tossed back, annoyed that she hadn't thought to look for such a thing.

'I want to talk to you about a few things—the hall particularly.'

'Oh, for heaven's sake,' she exclaimed impatiently. 'can't you see I'm busy preparing dinner?' It wasn't the way to talk to her employer, she knew, but at that moment she was too strung up about this first dinner. Closing the fridge door, she turned to look heatedly at him. 'It's important that you get to the table on time, so if you were intending to clean up——?' She paused suggestively and saw his eyes narrow, his mouth tighten to a hard line.

He breathed hard for a moment, then gave a brief nod and walked to the door. 'We'll talk about it later.'

Joanna stared at the door after his broad shoulders had disappeared beyond it. What was he so mad about? He had mentioned the hall, but surely he could find nothing to fault there. Perhaps his gimlet eyes had dis-

covered a smear of mud she had overlooked ... or perhaps he was always giving off that air of disapproval,
maybe bad temper was habitual with him. In which
case, she wondered that the woman he was supposedly
building the new house for, the one he had been engaged
to once before, was contemplating taking him on again
as a marriage partner. What had Liz said her name was?
Erikson ... Paula Erikson.

Her thoughts continued as she whisked the eggs into
a pale yellow froth. Physically Alex was an attractive
man, with the bigness that could spell security for a small
girl like herself ... or it could be overwhelmingly threat-
ening, she supposed, depending on how he regarded a
person. For a moment last night, when his fingers had
lifted her chin to face his searching look, she had sensed
another side to him. A purely male sensuality that had
sent an answering shiver through her.

Shaking herself mentally, Joanna returned her attention to the meal she was preparing, and thoughts of Alex
Harper's desirability or lack of it faded from her mind.

Promptly at seven she manoeuvred a large tray through
the two doors into the hall, and moments later was laying an attractive shrimp cocktail at each place, standing back to admire the effect on the elegant table. The
shrimps were canned, to be sure, but nestled on lettuce
over beds of crushed ice, they looked as professional
as any she had seen in the best restaurants.

'Very pretty,' a mocking voice said behind her, and
she spun round to see Alex approaching with a lazy
stride from the doorway. He was transformed from
a dusty-looking working man into one of casually well-
dressed prosperity. A silky pale yellow turtleneck sweater
blended well with nut brown tailored slacks and highly
polished brown casual shoes. He must have a fetish about

polished leather, Joanna thought abstractedly as he moved closer and brought with him a drift of spicy lotion from his newly shaved chin.

His eyes flickered round the table. 'You didn't do as I told you and set a place for yourself,' he remarked tautly.

Indicating her own appetiser on the buffet, Joanna said: 'I was about to do it.' Unaccountably nervous, she schooled her fingers not to tremble weakly as she brought cutlery from the buffet and started to arrange it round the cocktail.

'Not there, for God's sake! Balance up the table and set it at this end.' Irritably he indicated with an impatient hand the place opposite his own at the head of the table.

'But that's——'

'For the lady of the house?' he finished silkily, going with his easy stride to the top of the table and pulling out his chair. 'Don't fill your pretty little head with unrealistic dreams, Miss Thomas.' He smiled grimly as he sat down, adding in a lower tone: 'But it should be fun watching you try to fill that chair on a permanent basis.'

Joanna's breath expelled itself in a gasp at his arrogant assumption that she must surely regard him as a prize worth catching, but she had no time to reply as Nick and Glen came into the room at that moment.

After a protracted silence, when neither of them sat down or spoke, she looked up from where she was arranging the cutlery to see the thunderstruck looks on their faces as their eyes went over the table. Glen was the first to find his voice.

'I think we must have come to the wrong place, Nick,' he said, awed. 'This can't be our rough and ready table.'

Nick seemed about to agree, but a glance up at

Joanna's face as he pulled out his chair and sat down made him say quietly:

'It looks beautiful, Anna. We haven't had as nice a table since our mother died.'

Joanna, seated by now, murmured something which she felt was inadequate to express her thanks to Nick, the one she had named 'Peacemaker.' His gentle manners were something his brothers could learn from, she thought sourly, lifting her fork to the cocktail and venturing a look across the table to Alex's face. She was surprised at the thoughtfulness she saw there, but almost immediately a smile of mockery curved his mouth.

'And as you've gone to the trouble of bringing out the Jacobean crystal glasses our mother brought back from a visit to Scotland some years ago, I think I should make an effort to find some wine to fill them.'

Before getting up, however, he rapidly dispensed with the shrimps and lettuce, giving the impression that he could have tossed off a dozen more cocktails without impairing his appetite one bit.

Joanna escaped to the kitchen with the dishes and breathed a sigh of relief at the sight of a complacently risen soufflé behind the glass viewing door of the oven. Taking the bread rolls, which she had discovered that morning in a huge freezer located in the laundry room along the passage, from the warming oven above the stove, she wrapped them in a clean linen towel already arranged in a round wicker backet she had found. Next came the huge wooden bowl of tossed salad, and lastly the transfer of the precious soufflé in its dish to the tray.

Nick sprang gallantly to his feet when she entered the dining room and took the heavy tray from her. Glen looked momentarily sheepish, as if his brother's act laid guilt on himself, but Alex continued pouring ruby wine into the exquisitely cut glasses at each place.

Joanna stifled the involuntary remark that sprang to her lips. The richness of red wine would destroy the delicate flavour of the soufflé, but it was apparent to her that in this all-male household, wine was not a usual accompaniment to a meal. White wine was probably non-existent in the house and besides, Alex had already opened the bottle of red. The label was one she recognised as an excellent one, and she spared a glance for the tall rancher as he reseated himself and looked appraisingly at the food they were about to consume. Was it her imagination, or did his lips tighten in a way that was becoming only too familiar to her?

Turning quickly back to the soufflé, Joanna cut into it and saw its height diminish rapidly. Unfortunately, it seemed to have stuck to the glass dish, and by the time she had served wedges of it to each plate it resembled a shrivelled pancake more than the soaring perfection it had been minutes before.

She bit down hard on her lip when Alex accepted the plate Glen handed to him and stared down at the minuscule offering in grim-faced silence. Then, moving like a man in great pain, he helped himself liberally to the salad and took two rolls from the basket at his elbow. His brothers followed suit, and there was silence for several minutes while they crunched on crisp vegetables and chewed on the now rubbery soufflé.

Three hands reached at once for the two remaining rolls. Joanna herself, having seen that the brothers evidently enjoyed the warm rolls, had passed up the two she had allotted for herself.

'You wouldn't by chance have more rolls warming in the kitchen, I suppose?' Alex drawled, withdrawing from the contest and allowing his younger brothers to empty the wicker basket.

'I—well, no,' Joanna returned blankly. 'I allowed two for each of us.' Her tone implied that two should be enough for any normal person, and Alex sighed in a curiously gentle way.

'I see. Is there—something more to come?'

'Of course. I'll bring in dessert now.'

She rose and collected the plates, replacing them on the tray with the chilled melon slices she had previously prepared, and plugging in the electric coffee maker before returning to the dining room.

The excited hum of male voices ceased abruptly when she made her appearance, and she wondered if the brothers had been talking about the subject that seemed dearest to men's hearts—women. Glen's half guilty flush seemed to confirm that assumption, and Nick seemed too effusive in his thanks when she placed the melon wedge before him. Alex's lips seemed to tighten just a bit more as he gazed down at the pale fruit in front of him.

'Coffee should be ready when we've finished this,' Joanna said cheerfully as she sat down, elated to know that her first meal at Clearwater was safely behind her.

The soufflé hadn't exactly been a success, she mused, but the men had shown their appreciation of the meal by emptying the vast salad bowl and the roll basket, and eating every scrap of the shrimp cocktails. Complacently, she looked around at the males who were already beginning to feel like her own.

'I'm sure you're not always as quiet as this,' she said brightly to the table at large. 'Please don't let me stop you talking in the normal way, I'm sure you have lots of things to talk over about the ranch.'

Three pairs of brown eyes of varying intensity re-

garded her blankly for a moment or two, then Nick
looked at Alex and said in a constricted tone:

'What's on for tomorrow?'

Alex cleared his throat. 'Er ... mmm ... well, I
thought we'd tackle the northern pastures, check the
branding corrals ...'

'You're going to be *branding* cattle?' Joanna interrupted wide-eyed.

'That's the general intention,' Alex returned drily,
going on to elaborate: 'Though most of that's done in
the fall after round-up. The few we'll be doing now are
the ones we missed last fall.'

'But I thought that went out years ago, with rustlers
and lawless cowboys.'

'Rustling still hasn't disappeared,' he drawled, pushing away the glass dessert plate and taking one of the
cigars lined up in his breast pocket. 'But we bring the
cows in for other reasons, too. They have to be inocu-
lated against infection, and then there's——'

'Alex!' warned Nick, his voice low and his eyes on
the melon rind before him.

Alex glanced at him in amusement, then shrugged as
he applied a match to his cigar. 'Sorry, I forgot you're
a green city girl with matching sensitivity. We don't see
many of those around here,' he drew on the cigar and
expelled a cloud of azure smoke towards the ceiling
before looking directly at Joanna and added with narrow
eyed deliberation: 'apart from the ones Liz sicks on to
us.'

Joanna stared back into the mocking brown of his
eyes, then pushed back her chair. 'I'll get the coffee,' she
said with dignity, and collected the last set of dishes
before escaping once more to the kitchen.

Arrogant pig! Full of his own importance and su-

premely confident of his attraction to the opposite sex. It
was high time he took a tumble, and she, Joanna Thomas,
might be just the one to start him on that downward
roll. How or when she didn't know, but she'd do it or
die in the attempt.

She was approaching the dining room with the coffee
when Glen's facetiously raised voice stilled her feet.

'I know one person who won't be happy about you
having a way-out chick like Anna sitting opposite you
at the table every night.'

'Which person would that be?' Alex asked quietly.

Before Glen had a chance to answer, Joanna swept
into the room with the tray and desposited it with a
thud on the table. 'He probably means Miss Erikson ...
Paula, isn't it?'

Alex's head jerked back as if she had struck him, his
eyes narrowing to slits again as he stared down the table
at her. At last he said slowly:

'Liz really did your homework for you, didn't she?'

'She told me you were building a love-nest here for
Paula, if that's what you mean,' Joanna threw back
boldly, handing round the coffee she had poured into
fine china cups, scarcely seeing the quick flash of Alex's
eyes between Nick and Glen.

'You could say that.' The words were a drawn-out
drawl.

'Are you really building that place for Paula?' Nick
asked curiously, seeming deflated when his older brother
replied with a laconic:

'Who else? Don't you think it's her kind of place?'

Nick gave a noncommittal shrug. 'I guess so, she likes
new things, but—hell, Alex, you don't! You've always
seemed more than happy with the old place.'

'A change is as good as a rest, they say,' Alex shrugged

in his turn, 'and the lady concerned should be considered, wouldn't you say?'

It was then that the idea struck Joanna ... so forcibly that she had to consciously loosen her grip on the delicate china handle of her cup.

Alex was obviously in love with this Paula, or he wouldn't be building the shrine of her choice. Suppose she, Joanna, put a temporary spoke in their wheel? For a fleeting moment last night she had sensed that, given the right circumstances, Alex wouldn't be averse to kissing her. She wasn't unattractive and he might even fall a little in love with her. Only a little ... that would suffice to send his arrogant pride tumbling at the inevitable time when she would scornfully reject him.

Paula Erikson would know nothing about it, and therefore wouldn't be hurt ... although a woman who broke her engagement to a man simply because he had been saddled with the upbringing of younger siblings deserved her own come-uppance, Joanna mused.

'What schemes are you hatching now?'

Alex's dry question sliced into her thoughts and she looked up and blinked, realising that Nick and Glen had taken their leave and only Alex remained, staring lazily down the table at her with half-closed eyes.

Violet rested on brown for only a moment before Joanna's gaze shifted intently to the coffee pot beside her. 'S-schemes? I don't know what you—would you like more coffee?'

'Bring it to me,' he commanded softly, watching her as she came round the table to fill his cup from the pot.

Her eyes flew open in shock when his arm caught her round the waist and drew her to him so that her knees pressed against the firm muscles of his thigh. With his other hand, he removed the coffee pot from her lifeless fingers and placed it on the table.

'Now,' he said, his brow wrinkled thoughtfully as he gazed up into her eyes, 'would you tell me one thing? Is that stutter you have on occasion a congenital thing, or is it something that only happens when you're tired?'

'S-stutter?'

'You just did it again,' he said patiently. 'What is it? Are you afraid of me or something? You don't do it when you talk to Nick or Glen.'

'Afraid of you?'

Joanna blinked her black lashes in an effort to disentangle her gaze from his, but when she focused again the brown eyes, suddenly warm, looked implacably into hers.

'Don't keep repeating everything I say,' he commanded in a softly husky tone, his warm breath on her skin the only indication that she was now sitting on those firm thighs. His arm, still around her, was like a steel band of muscle. Dreamlike, she felt herself swaying towards the sensuous line of his lips.

This was what she had wanted, wasn't it? she asked herself dazedly. To trap this man into a loosely woven web of love, of desire, her final triumph being her scornful rejection of him.

But somehow, as the sensitive fullness of her lips met the firm outline of his, those thoughts took flight and left her alone to solve the inexplicable dilemma of a heart that suddenly beat too rapidly, of lips that sought vainly to capture and hold the teasing lightness of his. Her hand rose unconsciously to brush through the thickness of his hair in an effort to hold his head steady, but there was immediate resistance against her fingers.

'If it's any consolation to you,' Alex murmured against her mouth, 'you've got further in a shorter time than any of Liz's other hopefuls.'

When the words penetrated her brain, Joanna sat up abruptly on his knee. 'You love yourself, don't you?' she scorned as she pulled herself up and away from him. The returning clarity in her mind informed her that in this first real skirmish, he had won hands down.

'Not half as much as you girls love the thought of spending all the money you think I have,' he drawled, a cynical smile lifting a corner of his mouth.

'Money doesn't interest me,' Joanna told him loftily, lifting the coffee pot and returning to her own seat. Looking down the table at him suspiciously as she poured coffee into her cup, she asked: 'Who are all these girls you keep talking about, anyway? Is your sister in the habit of sending temporary housekeepers out here?'

'I hope you know how to get coffee stains out of tablecloths,' he observed mildly, and Joanna realised with a horrified glance downwards that the pot she had poured from automatically had filled not only the cup but the saucer, and dark coffee was seeping into the pristine whiteness of the linen cloth. With a smothered exclamation, she pushed the cup aside and thrust her napkin under the cloth as she had seen countless maids do when her young fingers had made spills.

'I'd advise you to see to that right away,' Alex said from above her head. 'And when you've done that and stacked the dishes in the machine, come and find me in the study. I have a few things to say to you.'

Fuming, Joanna cleared away the coffee things on to the tray, then whipped off the offending cloth, bundling it under her arm and balancing the tray with difficulty on her way out to the kitchen. Once there, she opened up the tablecloth and stared perplexedly at the brown stain that seemed to have enlarged enormously. 'I hope you know how to get coffee stains out of tablecloths,' she mimicked Alex's voice silently. Not for the world would she have told him that she had never removed any kind of stain from anything.

It couldn't be too difficult. Filling one of the double sinks with cold water, she plunged the stained section of cloth into it and left it to soak while she went to tackle the dishwasher. She had intended doing the dishes by hand as she had despatched the breakfast things this morning, but Alex would come looking for her if she ignored his summons for too long.

Actually, it seemed just a simple commonsense machine, with sections for different sized plates and prongs on the upper level obviously meant for cups and glasses. A row of dials along the top gave a choice of washes and the soap container was clearly marked.

The machine was soon loaded, and Joanna looked complacently at the neatly stacked rows of plates below and cups and glasses above before closing the door and pulling the start button. There was a satisfying hum of activity behind the door immediately, and she hurried back across the kitchen to check on the tablecloth.

Biting her lip, she looked down at the stain, as dark brown as ever. Maybe she should have used hot soapy water, the cold seemed to have set it faster than ever. The frown wrinkling her brow cleared suddenly when she remembered a large green container she had seen that morning in the supply room. It had been labelled 'Heavy Duty Bleach' and surely that would do the trick of removing the stain.

Skidding lightly along to the storage room, she staggered back to the kitchen with the heavy container, ignoring the instructions for use when she discovered they were for making up vast quantities of solution. A

reference to the cleaning and disinfecting of farm buildings had her breathing a sigh of relief. If the stuff would
clean a pigsty, it would certainly go a long way towards
removing a simple stain on a tablecloth.

Guessing at the quantity, she tipped the heavy container and poured the solution directly on to the cloth,
and was gratified when the stain miraculously began to
disappear before her eyes. Deciding to leave it to soak,
she went to find out what Alex had to say.

After returning the bleach container to the storeroom,
Joanna slipped into her bedroom and renewed her make-
up, then on a whim loosened her hair which had been
severely caught back during the dinner hour. Her first
try at temporarily ensnaring Alex Harper had been a
dismal failure, but he might be more mellow now that
he had eaten and had a chance to relax.

But relaxation seemed far from his mind when she
opened the study door and found him bent over the large
desk, frowning as he scanned the top sheet of a pile of
papers, then scrawled hurriedly on the open cheque
book before him.

At last he looked up, as if only then becoming aware
of her presence.

'Bills,' he grimaced, throwing down his pen and rising to stretch wearily. 'The world can fall down around
us, but the bills still keep coming.' For a moment his
eyes were warm as they went lazily over her silky cloud
of black hair and down to the blue sheath that emphasised the curves and indentations of her petite figure.
Something flared briefly in his eyes, but by the time they
had returned to her face the warm brown had changed
to coolness.

'You said you wanted to see me,' Joanna began, 'but
if you're busy ...'

'It's more important that I set you straight on a few things,' he clipped, coming round the desk and startling her by taking her arm in a firm grip to guide her to the door.

In the hall, he stopped by the long centre table and released her. 'See anything wrong with this floor?'

'The floor?'

Bewildered, Joanna stared at the red and grey tiles beneath their feet. Her eyes moved further and discerned a faint—very faint—line of demarcation between cleaned area and the balance of the hall.

'You're joking,' she lifted her head to say, and saw the swift shake of his.

'There's nothing funny about a job sloppily done. I don't tolerate that from the ranch employees outside, and I certainly won't from you.

'In future, you'll mop this floor every other day, and scrub and wax it on Fridays. And there's another thing ...' He took her arm again and led her back to the study and across to the closed door of his bedroom. Opening it with a flourish, he thrust her ahead of him and demanded: 'To what you tell me is your experienced eye, does anything seem amiss in here?'

Joanna's eyes flickered mutinously round the room with its dark furniture, then she said sulkily: 'You haven't made your bed.'

'Correction. *You* haven't made my bed. Making beds isn't my thing, that's why I employ a housekeeper.'

Before Joanna had time to make a reply, his arm had imprisoned her elbow again and she was wheeled back into the study and seated unceremoniously in a padded chair by the desk.

'I realise that your first day has been a difficult one, with no one to show you around and tell you what's expected of you, but that's why I asked you to come in here. To tell you that ... oh, hell,' he ran a hand through the thick russet of his hair, 'the laundry baskets are overflowing, there's dust on every surface you can see, and ... I'm starving,' he ended starkly.

Joanna blinked, then stared across the desk at him. 'But you just ate!'

'I ate the kind of meal a man who works at a desk job might find satisfactory,' he elaborated in a strained voice. 'Have you any idea how hungry a man gets after a long and very hard day's work in the open air?'

'Your brothers seemed happy enough with the meal I gave them,' she returned stiffly, 'and they're outdoor men too.'

Alex leaned forward across the desk and said with an almost frightening intensity: 'I'd bet everything I have that Nick and Glen are in the kitchen right now making themselves the biggest goddam sandwiches you ever saw.' His head moved to one side in an attitude of listening. 'Come with me,' he said urgently, and leapt round the desk to pull Joanna to her feet and drag her to the door, which he opened cautiously before pulling her forward to see through the crack.

Climbing the stairs, with remarkable stealth for well-set men, were Nick and Glen, loaded plates clutched in their hands. Joanna felt nauseous, betrayed, as she turned back into the room.

'All right,' she said testily, 'you've made your point. If stodge is what you want, then stodge is what you'll get. Tomorrow night you'll have potatoes coming out of your ears and—and deep dish apple pie loaded with pastry.'

'Mm ...!' he groaned with such bared longing in his eyes that she marched to the door.

'Is there anything else?'

'No ... no, I don't believe so.'

Her temper had evaporated very little when she reached the kitchen, but she stood beside the table there and looked contemplatively at the fridge. If Nick and Glen were hungry enough to raid it, then Alex must be too. Honesty compelled her to admit that the unaccustomed business of the day had left her with a sinking feeling around her own midriff.

Shrugging irritatedly, she went to the fridge and removed a sadly diminished ham and the remains of the cleaned salad ingredients she had used for dinner. Ten minutes later she made her way back to the study with a tray on which reposed a many-layered sandwich of gigantic proportions and re-heated coffee from the dinner pot.

Her peremptory tap at the door was answered by an uncharactertstically subdued: 'Come in' and a strange kind of pleasure surged through her when Alex looked up from the desk, his eyes widening incredulously when she placed the tray within his reach.

'Anna? What the——?'

'You said you were hungry.' She dismissed his amazement by crossing to his bedroom door. 'Maybe that will hold you till your breakfast steak.'

'Steak?'

'Must you repeat everything I say?' she triumphantly echoed his own words to her, and turned the handle of the door. 'I'm about to earn my housekeeping wages by making your bed.'

There was reward for her in the brief glimpse she caught of his confounded expression, but the feeling was shortlived as she busied herself in remaking the double-sized bed. Making beds was one task she had been taught to do neatly and well at school, but there was a puzzled frown on her brow as she plumped up the pillows and smoothed the bedspread over them. She bent to look under the bed, then crossed to the chest of drawers near the door and rifled quickly through its disordered contents.

'Looking for something?' a laconic drawl came from the door, and she looked pink-cheeked to see Alex leaning nonchalantly against the frame as if he had been there for some time.

'I can't seem to find your pyjamas,' she said.

'That's not surprising. I don't use them.'

'You don't——?'

'I sleep in the raw,' he informed her solemnly, but there was a gleam far back in his eyes. 'Haven't you ever tried it? Oh, no,' softly, 'you wear very sexy nightdresses, don't you?'

The colour flamed to brightness under her skin, but Joanna collected herself with commendable speed. 'You should know!' she said tartly, and went to sweep by him. 'You invaded my privacy this morning.'

He caught her round the waist as she flounced past, pulling her close to the long hard line of his lazily propped body. His other hand came up to smooth the silken strand of black hair from her face.

'And I'll invade it again tomorrow morning,' he murmured, his mouth so close that she felt the disturbing warmth of his breath on her skin, 'if you're not up to cook my breakfast.'

Joanna's tone was frigid. 'That won't be necessary. Your regular housekeeper left an alarm clock behind, so I'll be up bright and early.' Awareness of his stark male appeal as he pressed her body to his made her voice less steady, and she abruptly abandoned her essay at seduction. Some deep-seated instinct told her that she would be the loser in that kind of game.

'Pity,' was Alex's only comment, but his eyes seemed to darken as they went over her hair and rested on the full curve of her lips. Reluctantly, Joanna felt herself drawn again to the firm cut of his mouth, felt the yielding softness of her own body against his hard flesh, and wondered for a dizzy moment what it would be like if he kissed her and meant it.

But that reminded her of the light teasing of his lips in the dining room and his subsequent arrogance about her duties, and she pulled away from him to walk briskly into the study.

'If there's nothing else you need, I'll say goodnight,' she said from the door, turning back and surprising a vaguely puzzled look around his eyes as he lounged back into the room.

'Playing it cool to start with, hm?' He smiled with lazy approval. 'Smart girl ... though all I wanted to do was to show my appreciation for your thoughtfulness.' He indicated the untouched sandwich on his desk.

'Am I to expect a similar method of expressing thanks from your brothers?' she asked acidly, feeling a surge of satisfaction when his eyes narrowed in irritation.

Evenly, he said: 'Hardly. Nick's already spoken for and I doubt if his fiancée would appreciate his dallying with the housekeeper. And Glen's a little young for you, isn't he?'

'Two years' difference in age means nothing these days,' Joanna tossed back, feeling a savage need to hurt him for his snobbish remark about Nick and the housekeeper. 'Anyway, don't you think your own fiancée would object to your dallying with the hired help?'

'I don't have a fiancée.'

'Then who are you building the new house for?'

'Ah ... I didn't say I had no prospects of acquiring a fiancée in the near future.'

Joanna stared back at him in impotent rage, though why she should feel so incensed was beyond her. She was here at Clearwater in the role of housekeeper, and if Alex Harper produced a dozen fiancées it was none of her business.

'Bully for you,' she contented herself with saying, 'or should I say bully for her? According to you, she's captured the prize of the Cariboo, lucky girl.'

Alex moved so swiftly she had time to do no more than draw the door open before he was beside her.

'She'll think so, I assure you,' he said, his voice softly menacing. 'But in the meantime, maybe you should direct all that venomous energy into taking care of the house as I've instructed. As I told you last night, I intend to see to it that you earn your pay.'

'Don't worry, I'll earn every penny of it,' she snapped, and almost leapt away from him into the hall. Her breath was still pumping through her lungs in short angry gasps when she whirled into the kitchen and saw the tablecloth still soaking in the sink.

'Every rotten penny of it,' she muttered as she crossed to the sink and tugged irritably at the sodden mass.

Seconds later she was staring, horrified, at the tablecloth suspended between her hands. The stain had gone completely—but so had the linen under it. The gaping hole enlarged itself when she convulsively parted it between her hands, and her nerveless fingers dropped it back into the searing solution in the sink.

How could she have been so stupid as to have poured that unknown quantity of caustic bleach on to it? Her breath caught on a half sob as she visualised Alex's grim expression of 'I thought as much' when he knew about it.

*If* he knew about it, she told herself feverishly. There were several cloths in different colours in the buffet drawers. She could send an emergency call to Liz to buy another white one and send it to her ... the men were out most of the day, so she would receive the parcel herself.

With the steel of desperation, Joanna rolled up the tablecloth, wettest part inside, and released the telltale solution from the sink. As a temporary measure, she carried it to her own bathroom and dropped it into the tub. Time enough tomorrow to think of its final disposal.

Back in the kitchen, she sank weakly on to a chair and leaned her head on her hands. A disaster such as the ruined tablecloth could be devastating ammunition in Alex Harper's hands ... he might even change his mind about holding her here to do the job he had hired her to do. And the thought of that filled her with despair.

She hated his arrogant self-assured ways, but some inner sensitivity told her that she would make it here or not at all. Joanna's last stand, she told herself wryly. Or she would go back to Vancouver and drift into marriage with someone suitably endowed with worldly goods, as befitted her father's daughter.

Her eyes fell on the now quiescent dishwasher. Wearily, she decided that she might as well put away the dishes tonight. Tomorrow promised to be a busy day if Alex had his autocratic way.

The dinner plates were sparkling clean on the lower level, and Joanna felt a glow of satisfaction as she stacked them tidily into the cupboards above the washer. The cutlery, too, sparkled cleanly as she scooped it from the individual containers and laid it out on the counter ready to take into the dining room.

It was when she slid out the top tray of the washer that her heart seemed to plummet and stop entirely.

'Oh, dear God, no ... you couldn't let this happen to me!' she whispered disbelievingly.

But it had happened. Every one of the four glasses, the Jacobean crystal which the Harper mother had brought back from Scotland, swung drunkenly on its peg, broken-off sections glinting mockingly up at her from the basket below.

# CHAPTER FIVE

'THIS coffee's a little cold, Anna. Is there any chance of——? Good God, what in hell——?'

Joanna lifted her stricken eyes to the stern white line of Alex's jaw. 'I—I'm sorry,' she whispered, 'I—I'll replace them.'

'Just how are you going to do that?' he asked starkly, raising bleak eyes to meet the distressed blue of hers. 'How do you know that the Craigmillar pattern is still available, even if you should be able to send to Scotland for them?'

'Cr-Craigmillar? I'm sure they're still making them... I'll get replacements, Alex,' she said feverishly. 'I know it won't mean the same as the set your mother brought back, but ...'

'Forget it,' he said tautly, turning on his heels. 'And forget the coffee, too!'

Tears welled up in her eyes and overflowed as his incensed figure stamped from the kitchen. It just wasn't fair that so many things should go wrong on her first day.

First day! It seemed as if a year had gone by since Alex had forded the raging torrent of the previous night. How brave he had been, how uncaring for his own safety but watchful of hers! And she had rewarded him by shattering the precious symbol of his dead mother's travels.

Choking back sobs, she raced to her bedroom and tugged a writing pad from the top drawer of the dresser. Raking feverishly through her handbag, she unearthed the list of her father's movements on his combined business and honeymoon trip. Clearing the tears from her blurred eyes, she saw that his three-day stopover in Edinburgh was for the seventeenth of the month. Plenty of time for a letter to reach him at his hotel.

Sniffing as she wrote, she penned:

'Dearest Daddy and Marie: I hope you're enjoying your trip so far. I can't wait to hear all about it when you come back.

'Sorry I'm in such a rush, but could you possibly find out if there's such a thing as "Craigmillar" crystal still being made in Edinburgh? I'm staying with the family of an old school friend here in the Cariboo, and I'd like to replace some crystal wine glasses that were broken accidentally. They were brought back from Scotland years ago by my friend's mother, now dead, so naturally they're upset at the breakage.

'If you can send four to *Anna* Thomas at the above address, and please use a name like John Smith as the sender, I'll love you for ever. But you know I'll do that anyway! I'll explain all this when I see you again. Have fun, love you both, Joanna.'

She knew that if such a brand of crystal was obtainable in Scotland, James Thomas would make sure the glasses reached her in the remote interior. And he was well enough versed in the idiosyncrasies of his daughter to fall in with her wishes as to the mailing instructions. By the time he and Marie returned from their honeymoon trip, the regular housekeeper at Clearwater would be back in harness and Joanna herself back in the city.

Somehow, the latter thought brought her little pleasure.

'Do you ride, Anna?'

Glen asked the question at breakfast the next morning, but it was Alex's face Joanna's eyes flew to. He had made no remark about the steak, eggs and crisp bacon she had placed before him when he returned to the house after his early morning foray into ranch chores.

He had seemed remote, abstracted in his manner—perhaps still brooding about the shattered glasses which had been a memento of his mother. Joanna had an aching longing to tell him that if it were possible to have them replaced, her father would do so. But she couldn't say that. An unemployed factory worker would hardly be taking an extended tour of Europe.

'What?' she murmured abstractedly when Glen spoke again. 'Oh ... well, not many people have a chance to ride in the city.'

'I guess not,' Glen said in a commiserating voice, adding eagerly: 'I could teach you, though! It's great to get on a horse and just take off, Anna, and——'

Now Alex came to life. Coldly, he interrupted: 'You have altogether too much work to do to think of teaching a greenhorn to ride, and Anna has enough to keep her occupied indoors.' Or should have, his tone implied.

'I'm not really bothered about riding anyway,' Joanna flared slightly, then smiled at Glen's concerned young face. 'But thanks!'

Glen's expression reflected unrest as he glared at his older brother. 'You don't expect her to stay chained to the house all the time, do you?'

Amusement tinged Alex's wry: 'I don't recall that you ever worried about Martha being chained to the house! But then her waistline just about matched her age, didn't it?'

'You're really rotten sometimes, Alex, you know that?' Glen's light skin showed bright red, clashing with the carroty hue of his hair.

'Yeah.' Unperturbed, Alex pushed away his chair and stood up. 'Let's go. There's a lot to do today.'

'And every day,' Nick said *sotto voce* as he rose too and scraped his chair back under the table. The smile he gave Joanna was half apologetic. 'Thanks for breakfast, Anna, it was great.'

When they had clumped off—like the three bears, she thought irreverently—Joanna sank down on a kitchen chair and peacefully savoured a freshly poured coffee. Of the three brothers, she mused, Nick had to have the nicest nature, gentle, kind and with an attractive touch of shyness. She hoped that Shirley, his fiancée, was the kind of girl who really appreciated his fine qualities.

It was later that morning, in the midst of sponge mopping the vast hall, that she had an opportunity to find out. Lost in her thoughts, she just distantly heard a light voice calling: 'Hello?' from the kitchen.

Before she had time to do more than immerse the mop in the bucket and turn round, a slender fair-haired girl was silhouetted in the doorway. Of about her own age, the girl had fine blonde hair fringed over her brow and cut so that it fell straight down to curve under her chin. Eyes of a lighter blue than Joanna's looked ready to twinkle into a smile at any moment, a pert nose was was sprinkled generously with pale freckles, and a mouth which, like the eyes, seemed made for smiling. A blue checked shirt topped close-fitting blue jeans round slender hips.

If Joanna's appraising eyes were surprised, the other girl's were doubly so as they went over dark hair contrasted with the stark white of a wrap-around work apron which, despite its size, did little to hide the trim contours of her figure.

'Are *you*—the new housekeeper?' the girl asked faintly.

'That's right, J—Anna Thomas,' she corrected just in time. 'And you're——?'

'Shirley Ames ... Nick and I are engaged.'

'Oh, that's great. I was wondering a little while ago just what you were like.'

'You were?' Shirley looked doubtfully at Joanna as she left the work bucket and came towards her with a smile.

'Yes, Nick's so nice, I hoped you were too.' Joanna offered a faintly damp hand and added: 'Can you stay for coffee?'

'Well ...' the other girl's eyes moved back to the unfinished floor, 'you seem to be busy. I just called by to say Hi and introduce myself.'

'I'm about due for a break,' Joanna dismissed the objection cheerfully, and led the way back to the kitchen, where she plugged in the percolator and busied herself with cups and saucers. 'You live some distance away, don't you?'

Shirley laughed and came forward to take a seat at the table. 'If you're used to city distances, I guess. Out here, we're next door neighbours.'

'I keep forgetting,' Joanna sighed, perking up when her eyes fell on a sleek bay gelding tethered a little distance from the house. 'She's a beauty,' she breathed wistfully, then turned back to Shirley. 'You rode over here?'

'Mm-hm. Do you ride? I suppose you must if you look like that just seeing Bunty from the window! She needed the exercise, and I did too.'

'Oh, I don't know too much about horses,' Joanna said hastily, taking a seat opposite the other girl. 'They're not something that city people have much knowledge of.'

'I guess not. It's a pity, though. You're pretty lost in country like this if you can't ride.'

'I can imagine.' Joanna looked bleak.

Shirley seemed to hesitate before speaking again. 'Have you—had many jobs like this? You seem too young to have had much experience ... and too good-looking to have to do it for a living,' she added in a rush. 'I mean, there must have been lots of men who wanted to——'

'I've never met anyone I'd care enough about to marry,' Joanna responded crisply, getting up to pour steaming coffee into their cups. *All they cared about was my father's money*, she added in desolated silence. Then, placing Shirley's coffee before her and seating herself with her own, she forced a smile across the table and said: 'But that's not your problem, is it? Before you came, I was thinking that Nick is quite the nicest one of the brothers.'

'You think so?'

The guarded tone of the other girl's voice shocked Joanna momentarily, then she leaned across the table to say earnestly: 'Listen, I only mean that ... well, I *like* him ... as a friend. That's why I hoped you were nice enough for him. And I think you are.'

Shirley smiled with a freeness that hinted of relief. 'Thanks. I hope you're right. I've been crazy about him since I was knee-high, and he didn't know I existed.' After a quick gulp of coffee, she smiled wryly. 'Anyway, I guess you'll be like most of the girls who come here, and fall for Alex. He's the masterful type most girls seem to love. One even told me that every time he looked in her direction, her knees almost buckled.'

'That was probably her money bone,' Joanna responded tartly, unconsciously repeating Alex's own summation of the females who came to Clearwater, including herself. 'Is he really that wealthy?'

'Well, the ranch alone is worth millions,' Shirley said artlessly, 'and Alex is well off apart from his lion's share in that. He's clever with investments and things like that.' Her brow crinkled thoughtfully. 'But I don't think it's just that that attracts girls to him. Don't you think he's very attractive in himself?'

'It sounds as if you're marrying the wrong brother!' Joanna prevaricated.

'Oh, no! I don't care that Nick doesn't have as much as Alex. In fact,' Shirley hesitated as if searching for words, 'Alex frightens me in a way. He's so—forceful, so strong. He'd expect so much from his wife ... brains, beauty, intelligence, and a high degree of competence in whatever she did—oh, I don't know. I'm just happy with Nick.'

'And that's how it should be,' Joanna said crisply, rising. 'By the way, even if I should fall for Alex, it wouldn't do me one bit of good. He thinks I'm the most incompetent creature to walk God's earth!'

'He does?'

'Definitely. You'll no doubt hear from Nick that I served mouse proportions for dinner to starving ranchers last night, and I was given a long list of duties I'd neglected to perform, ending with overflowing laundry hampers.'

Shirley grimaced. 'Oh, dear. Let me help you, Anna,' she added impulsively. 'I can at least get the laundry started for you. Really, I'd love to.'

'Well, if you're sure,' Joanna looked doubtfully at her. What would Alex have to say about his brother's fiancée helping out with the household chores?

'I'm sure. I don't have to get home for a couple of hours.'

Joanna needed no further encouragement. Already her limbs ached with the unaccustomed exertion of her muscles and rising from her bed hours earlier than normal.

In a surprisingly short space of time, the two girls were working in perfect harmony, although their spheres of operation differed. Shirley, hesitantly asking what Joanna had planned to serve for the evening meal, took a man-sized roast from the freezer and thoughtfully placed it in the sink to defrost under a gentle stream of cold tap water. Oddly, she seemed not to question Joanna's obvious incompetence, but seemed happy to have found a congenial friend.

By the time they sat down to a lunch prepared by Joanna, the hall floor sparkled with cleanliness and the furniture gleamed from the vigorous polishing it had received. Bedclothes were shaken out and beds remade smoothly with fresh linen, while a pile of clean laundry grew to massive proportions in the laundry room at the far end of the kitchen passage.

'I wish I could stay and do the ironing for you,' Shirley said regretfully over lunch, 'but I promised Mom I'd do some baking this afternoon. She hasn't been too well lately, so I help out as much as I can.'

'Do you have brothers and sisters?'

'Two brothers, but they're out on the ranch with Dad most of the time.'

'Married?'

'Josh, my older brother, is. Tim's still playing the field, like Glen.'

Josh, she told Joanna, was the father of twin boys.

'They're three, and you wouldn't believe the mischief they get into. Patsy has to have eyes in the back of her head.' She tipped her head to one side. 'You'll have to come over and meet everybody some time. Guaranteed headache at the end of the day.'

'I'd love to,' Joanna said gratefully, thankful for this newfound friend in an alien world. Then her face fell slightly. 'But I don't know when I'll be free.'

'You've got to have time off,' Shirley laughed disparagingly. 'Even Alex can't keep you with your nose to the grindstone every day of the week. I'll get Nick to bring you over one Sunday when the family's going to be there.' She looked thoughtful. 'Alex often goes over to the Erikson place on Sundays, and Glen spends most of his free time away from Clearwater, so you should be able to come.'

'Yes. Thanks.' With a falsely injected note of lightness, Joanna asked: 'Isn't Paula Erikson the one Alex is building the house for on the property?'

Shirley shrugged. 'It seems so, but I honestly can't see why Alex would want to marry her after what happened last time. They were engaged, you know, and then when Mr and Mrs Harper were killed so suddenly, Paula seemed to take fright at the thought of helping to bring up Alex's brothers and sister. I guess you've met Liz?' she went off on a tangent, accepting Joanna's assenting nod without further thought. 'Alex was just twenty-four, Nick twenty, the same age as Glen now, Liz eighteen and Glen fourteen. A pretty scary prospect, I suppose, for a girl.'

'I'd have done it,' Joanna said without thinking.

'So would I,' Shirley agreed simply. 'But Paula's a different breed. She's all those things I mentioned Alex would need in a wife—beautiful, intelligent, competent.

She rides a horse better than any other woman in the area, she can close a deal faster than any cattle dealer, and she's really beautiful—in a remote kind of way, know what I mean? I'm just glad she set her sights on Alex, not Nick, although she's closer to Alex's age than Nick's.'

'From the sounds of her,' Joanna smiled tightly, 'you've no need to worry.'

'No.' Shirley sighed thankfully, then rose. 'Thank goodness even her efforts to bring culture to the Cariboo haven't affected Nick at all.'

'Culture?'

'With a capital C,' Shirley returned gravely. 'Last year it was a well-known pianist, the year before a woodwind ensemble playing Elizabethan music by the hour. This year I hear it's to be Shakespeare.'

Joanna's footsteps faltered as she followed the other girl to the door. 'Shakespeare?' she asked faintly.

'Mmm. Alex seems to like it all—he always goes, anyway.'

'Oh.' Shakespeare ... what a strange coincidence. There could possibly be more than one Company doing Shakespeare in Vancouver. But Joanna knew there wasn't.

'Sure there's nothing else I can do for you before I go?' Shirley offered. 'Sorry I wasn't able to stay and do the ironing.'

'No reason why you should,' Joanna returned absently. 'It's my job, after all,' A sudden thought struck her. 'There *is* something you might do ... can you mail a couple of letters for me?'

Shirley laughed. 'Nothing easier. Being closer to town, we have a rural mailbox, but Clearwater's a little too far out so mail has to be taken in and collected in town.'

Joanna quickly fetched the letters from her bedroom, saying diffidently as she handed them over to the other girl: 'A distant relative of mine is on vacation in Scotland, and I promised I'd write. I also told Liz I'd let her know how things are going.'

Shirley followed her previous policy of not appearing too interested in Joanna's background, and simply glanced at the J. R. Thomas inscribed on one envelope before sliding the letters into her jacket pocket. Fortunately Joanna had brought a supply of stamps with her—and she hadn't really lied about the distance of her relative. Her father was far distant from her at the moment.

She stared thoughtfully, and somewhat enviously, after her visitor's slim figure mounted on the mare, Bunty. Shirley was the kind of girl it would be easy to make friends with ... more important, she was the ideal girl for Nick.

The days went by faster than they ever had before for Joanna, and she dropped into bed at night in a state of exhaustion that left little time for introspection before deep and dreamless sleep claimed her.

But at the end of her second week at Clearwater, she had a burgeoning sense of accomplishment in that she was slowly but surely mastering the details of running a house as large as the ranch. True, there had been several occasions when her inexperience had shown through, such as the ineradicable scorch on Alex's finest silk shirt on her first ironing spree—an occasion which brought a by now familiar tightness to his mouth but no caustic words, as if he was beyond finding them any more.

He did, however, present her silently with a thick glossy cookbook after a trip he made into town, and she learned from that, by trial and error. After that first roast, which had been seared outside and raw in the middle, she had gone on to serving the wholesome and dauntingly filling meals which the Harper men preferred to daintily served elegant suppers consisting mainly of salad greens and light entrees.

Then, while dusting in Alex's study one day, she had found, tucked away on a lower shelf in the bookcase, a handwritten recipe book. There was little in it to help in the preparation of basic meals, but there were annotations beside many of the recipes denoting which were the favourites of Anne Harper's husband and children.

One day she would surprise them all by making their favourite food, mainly dessert or cake recipes, which the unfortunate Anne had forever lost the power to do. Particularly the one marked 'Alex's favourite'—a dried fruit concoction between layers of pastry.

Another friend had come Joanna's way. Dusty, the well-named large dog she had seen greeting Alex rapturously on that first morning, had been summarily consigned to the ranch area. When Joanna could no longer bear the utter dejection of the disconsolate animal as she watched the men, especially her beloved master, ride out without her each morning, she enticed her into the house and comforted her with offerings of meaty bones from the night before's dinner, or scraps of whatever was left over.

Soon the animal clung as closely to her as it had done previously to Alex, following her about the house as she mopped and dusted and made beds. Some sixth sense told her to return the dog to the working area of the

ranch before Alex returned, and how right she had been
was demonstrated a week after she had befriended the
animal.

Alex came home early, alone, and strode into the
kitchen, pulling up short when his incredulous eyes
rested on the matlike form of the dog nestled close to
Joanna's feet under the table where she was preparing a
beef casserole, dropping an occasional titbit to the appreciative jaws below.

'What's she doing in here?' he barked, and the dog
slithered backwards under the table, away from his
wrathful glare.

'Don't blame her,' Joanna defended. 'She was so lonely
when you wouldn't take her out any more, so I let her
come in—and she's very happy with me.'

'I'm sure she is,' he said drily, advancing closer to the
table, and Joanna heard the quick scuffle of retreating
paws. 'Can't you see you're ruining her as a working
dog?'

'She *is* getting a little fatter,' Joanna admitted with
a downward glance at the obviously swelling sides. Then
she attacked: 'But what can you expect when you leave
her at home suddenly, without the exercise she's used
to?'

Alex sighed exasperatedly. 'I left her at home for the
same reason as there is for her bigger size. She's in pup.
And I doubt if your filling her to the brim with house
scraps is any better for her than my running her over
miles of rough terrain!'

'Oh.' Embarrassed colour swept up from Joanna's
neck to mantle her cheeks with bright pink. 'I didn't
know.'

'Obviously not. I'm taking her outside now, and she's
to stay in her own quarters, understood?'

'Yes,' she returned shortly, and felt her heart melt when the unfortunate Dusty came reluctantly from under the table at her master's peremptory tone, giving Joanna a reproachful look as she slunk, ears and tail down, after Alex's boots to the outdoors.

But watching from the window, Joanna reflected wryly on the perfidy of animal affections when she saw the disgraced Dusty rub ingratiatingly against the quickly striding male legs and reach up to the casually caressing hand on her head. Totally unpremeditated in her mind came the thought that Alex would have that same effect on women, a mindless desire to please his implacable maleness.

If the dog episode had ended there, no more trouble would have ensued, but Dusty had become used to her house coddling and, reluctant to give it up, presented herself to the back porch door every morning when the men had left, whining pleadingly every time Joanna made an appearance.

Compromising, Joanna fed her scraps from the porch door, forcing her to stay outside until, sensing Alex's return, the dog would disappear to receive his rough caress as he swung down from the saddle at the corral.

And then one morning Dusty didn't turn up. Joanna made frequent trips out to the grassy lawn behind the house, leaving the door open between forays so that she would hear the animal's plea for food and company, but the whole day passed without a sight of her.

Alex, too, had evidently missed her, for when he trooped in behind his brothers that evening, his eyes went in a questioning arc to Joanna.

'Have you see Dusty lately?'

'No.' Joanna's concern was reflected in the deep blue of her eyes as they met his across the kitchen table.

'She hasn't been in the house since I put her out?'

'No, of course not,' Joanna could say with truth. 'But I—I usually see her around during the day, and today she seems to have disappeared.'

Alex seemed relieved more than anything. 'Well, I guess she's found herself a cosy spot to have her pups. I'll check later.'

But later, when he returned from the work area, his brow had settled into a frown. He questioned Nick and Glen before they left the ranch, Nick to go to Shirley's place and Glen to the town attractions in Williams Lake, but neither of them had had sight nor sound of the missing dog.

'It's strange,' Alex pondered. 'I've never known her to stray far from the barns to have her pups.'

'Oh, she'll turn up in a day or so,' Glen said airily, fresh and youthfully sparkling in clean jeans and brightly coloured shirt that clashed with his vibrant hair.

His older brother looked appraisingly at him, the dog seemingly forgotten for the moment. 'Going out, Glen? I thought you'd decided to stay home and settle down at last.' His eyes flickered briefly over Joanna, and she compressed her mouth into a tight line.

'Yeah ... well,' embarrassed, Glen made for the front door, saying over his shoulder: 'I can't settle down till I've found a girl to do it with, can I? And I met this new chick in town last Saturday ... see you!'

'Just watch yourself in town,' Alex raised his voice to call after him. 'Remember——'

'You're not likely to let me forget, are you?' Glen retorted bitterly, and banged the door behind him.

Alex's mouth tightened fractionally, then he turned the warm brown of his eyes on Joanna, a derisive gleam lighting their depths.

'I was hoping your good influence would last a little longer than it has. I haven't even had to haul him out of bed once since you came.'

It was the first time he had referred even obliquely to their conversation that night in his study, and Joanna turned away to walk towards the kitchen.

'As you said, he's a little young for me.'

'True.' To her consternation, Alex followed her through the two doors and into the kitchen. They hadn't been alone in the house together since her first night there, and she felt edgy. Glen had been at home every night, evidently a record for him, except the previous Saturday when Alex himself had gone out dressed to eat dinner elsewhere. Nick, before leaving to spend the weekend at Shirley's home, had seemed the only one concerned about Joanna being left alone in the house.

'Why don't you come over with me, Anna?' he had asked diffidently. 'Shirley would love it, and her folks never mind how many people stay over. Alex and Glen can take care of themselves tomorrow. In fact, Glen might not come home at all, and Alex usually spends Sunday at the Erikson place. He's been buddies with Pete Erikson, Paula's brother, since they were tots.'

'Really?' Joanna had managed to suppress a derisive snort. Alex Harper hadn't struck her as the type who would spend nearly every Sunday with another man, not when there was an attractive woman present. And by all accounts Paula Erikson was that. 'No, please don't worry about me, Nick. Shirley asked me over one Sunday and I will, but right now I have a lot of catching up to do on personal things.'

So she had had the house to herself for virtually the whole weekend. Now that another was coming up, she didn't relish the thought of being alone in the big house which seemed like home only when Alex was in it—she caught herself up sharply and glanced briefly over her shoulder at his indolently draped figure just inside the door. His eyes seemed to be watching her closely in a way she couldn't fathom at that moment. Nervously, she smoothed the taut blue of her denim skirt over her hips.

'Would you—I-like some coffee?'

'I was beginning to think your stammer had improved along with your household skills,' he mocked softly, and came to where she stood by the table. 'Still scared of me?'

'I'm not scared of you,' she flared briefly up into his eyes, then let her own slide away to the opened neck of his shirt where more than a hint of reddish brown hair curled up towards his throat.

'Liar.' Casually his hands came up behind her head to pull loose the dark gloss of her hair confined by a white chiffon scarf. 'That's much better,' he murmured, running caressing hands over the silky strands and cupping her face to turn it up to his. 'Why have you been giving me the cold shoulder lately?'

Thinking he referred to the continual presence of either or both of his brothers, which had precluded any solitary exchange between them, Joanna breathed:

'Nick—Glen—are always around.'

'Ah, yes. Nick and Glen. But they're not here now, are they?'

His hands slid provocatively across her neck and did disturbing things to the soft yet firm flesh of her shoulders. In the same way, she felt a sudden yielding yet tautening of her stomach muscles, and she looked questioningly up at him, the full curve of her lips trembling in the uncontrollable shiver that ran through her body.

He was so big. The outline of his shoulders under pale

plaid shirt loomed over her smallness and seemed somehow menacing. But his mouth was smiling when he bent
his head to hers and touched her quivering lips, shocking
them into stillness.

Joanna had been kissed before ... but had she ever
been this aware of the potent hardness, the arrogant demand of a man's mouth? Or of the steel-banded muscles
of the lean body he moulded her to as the kiss deepened?

No, her dimly lit brain told her, this kiss was of a
quality she had never experienced before. The men who
had kissed her had bodies of cushioned softness far removed from the muscled tautness of this man, yet his
arms held her with a surprising gentleness that denied
the insistent probing of his mouth which at last parted
her lips and made coherent thought impossible.

Her own response to him was such that she felt nothing
but increased ardour when his supple fingers parted the
buttons on her blouse and explored the taut rise of her
flesh with hands roughened to abrasiveness by the nature
of his work. His mouth flamed a searing line across her
cheek to her ear and then descended to the column of
her throat, burning there for a moment or two before
resting briefly between her breasts. Then suddenly he
lifted his head and pushed her away from him in a dis-
missive gesture.

'You're just too small to make love to standing up,' he
said in a voice strange in its huskiness. His eyes held a
faint glimmer of puzzlement mingled with rapidly dying
passion as his hands encircled her wrists and drew her
arms from around his neck ... and she hadn't even been
aware of their tight clutch there until he did so.

'And taking you to bed,' he went on in a deliberate
drawl, 'would be falling in with my sister's and your
plans more neatly than I care for. Though I must admit,'

he heaved a gigantic and faintly regretful sigh, 'you almost had me nailed to the post there!'

Fumbling, Joanna's fingers found the opened buttons on her blouse and tremblingly closed them. Anger as much as recent passion had sent adrenalin careening through her veins.

'You're paranoid about your sister,' she threw at him from the safer distance of the sink, where she automatically filled the percolator and added coffee, plugging it into the socket without realising she was doing so. 'You've had the same housekeeper for years, so why do you keep trying to tell me that Liz has been sending housekeepers out here by the dozen?'

'Not as housekeepers,' he corrected, calmly buttoning his shirt which was open almost to the waist while Joanna watched the long fingers in horror-stricken shame. Had she done that? A fleeting remembrance of short harsh hairs against her palms told her that she must have, and her skin flooded with guilty colour. What could have possessed her?

Alex pulled out one of the chairs and straddled it, resting his arms along its back as he regarded her with steely amusement. 'Liz is getting more subtle in her strategy these days. The four or five others she's sent hotfoot down here to snare me have had much more obvious reasons for coming—a death in the family, which the open-air life at Clearwater would cure; overwork and the same cure; broken hearts—you name it, we've had them at Clearwater.'

'Whatever reasons Liz had for sending those others, it doesn't apply to me,' Joanna gritted through whitely clenched teeth. 'I came here to work! You can marry all the Paula Eriksons in the world for all I care.' She

# If you were in their place what would you do?

### Jeanette...

Though she has survived a heart-wrenching tragedy, is there more unhappiness in store for Jeanette? She is hopelessly in love with a man who is inaccessible to her. Her story will come alive in the pages of "Beyond the Sweet Waters" by Anne Hampson.

### Juliet...

Rather than let her father choose her husband, she ran...ran into the life of the haughty duke and his intriguing household on a Caribbean island. It's an intimate story that will stir you as you read "The Arrogant Duke" by Anne Mather.

### Laurel...

There was no turning back for Laurel. She was playing out a charade with the arrogant plantation owner. and the stakes were "love". It's all part of a thrilling romantic adventure called "Teachers Must Learn" by Nerina Hilliard.

### Fern...

She tried to escape to a new life...a new world...now she was faced with a loveless marriage of convenience. How long could she wait for the love she so strongly craved to come to her...Live with Fern...love with Fern...in the exciting "Cap Flamingo" by Violet Winspear.

**J**eanette, Juliet, Laurel, Fern...these are some of the memorable people who come alive in the pages of Harlequin Romance novels. And now, without leaving your home, you can share their most intimate moments!

It's the easiest and most convenient way to get every one of the exciting Harlequin Romance novels! And now, with a home subscription plan you won't miss *any* of these true-to-life stories, and you don't even have to go out looking for them.

You pay nothing extra for this convenience, there are no additional charges ...and you don't even pay for postage!

Fill out and send us the handy coupon now, and we'll send you 4 exciting Harlequin Romance novels absolutely FREE!

**A Home Subscription! It's the easiest and most convenient way to get every one of the exciting Harlequin Romance Novels!**

*...and you'll get 4 of them FREE*

## Get your
## *Harlequin Romance*
## Home Subscription NOW!

● Never miss a title! ● Get them first—
straight from the presses! ● No additional
costs for home delivery!
● These first 4 novels are yours—FREE!

**For exciting details,
see special offer inside.**

Printed in U.S.A.

stopped, aware from his knowing smile that she had fallen into his snare.

'If my sister's motives are as pure as you say they are,' he observed, 'it's surprising that she went into the details of my personal life so thoroughly.' His next question surprised Joanna. 'How long did you say you've known my sister?'

'Liz? Oh, n-not long. I just met her be-before she suggested I come here.'

'And why did she do that?' Alex leaned forward on the chair and said deliberately: 'A housekeeper you've never been, and Liz must have known that.'

'I told you—that first night—that Liz was kind enough to understand my—my circumstances,' Joanna faltered, her eyes not meeting the relentless probing of his. Her relief was limitless when the coffee percolator signalled its readiness. She jumped up and rushed to take cups from the cupboard. 'Will you have s-some coffee?'

'Y-yes, please,' he mimicked drily, and looked thoughtfully at her as she brought the steaming cups to the table, then arranged cream and sugar between them.

'Who are you, Anna? If that's your name,' he added softly, but the effect on Joanna was as if he had shouted at the top of his voice.

'Wh-what?'

'Do you really have a father who works in a factory and is unemployed right now?'

'Yes, I do,' she answered without prevarication, looking him straight in the eye. 'My father works in a factory, but he's not working right now.'

His eyes narrowed speculatively, but he drank some coffee before going on: 'And your parents were quite happy with the idea of your coming here to work as a housekeeper, although they knew nothing about us?'

'Why shouldn't they be?'

'I could have been a lecher for all they knew.'

Joanna's head reared back. 'And aren't you?' The soft rise of her breasts felt bruised from his handling a few minutes before.

He gave a low, and faintly mocking, laugh. 'Believe me, if I was you wouldn't be sitting there right now in all your innocence.'

'What makes you think I'm so innocent?' she challenged, lifting her chin to glare across at him. It would be the absolute last straw if he found fault with her response to his lovemaking on top of everything else. But Alex simply shrugged and said with a secretive kind of smile:

'Just a hunch I have. Would you have gone to bed with me a while ago?'

Her sharp 'No!' was instinctive, then she shrugged as he had said : 'Oh, well, why not? You're not exactly repulsive to me, as you must have known from how I reacted to you.'

He laughed in seeming enjoyment and drained his cup. Rising, he came round to chuck her under the chin. 'And you're not exactly repulsive to me, as *you* must have known from *my* reactions. But don't read too much into that, I'm just as normal as the next man.'

Oh no, you're not normal, Joanna thought when he had swung out of the kitchen to pursue whatever he had to pursue in the study. It was useless, she realised now, becoming incensed with his arrogance. If he was right— and she had no real reason to doubt him—Liz had been sending down a steady supply of prospective brides for his inspection, and he above all men wasn't the type to have his wife chosen for him by a younger sister. No, he would go his own way, marrying where it pleased him

... and it seemed as if the woman he was building the house for, Paula Erikson, was the one who pleased him.

And suddenly Joanna realised that that thought didn't please her at all. Unconsciously her fingers rose to touch the outline of her lips, which still throbbed from Alex's touch. Was it possible to fall completely in love with a man she had only known for a matter of weeks? With a sense of wonderment, she decided it was.

From the time of their meeting, she had been aware of him as a man, of his stubborn refusal to give in even to the elements. She saw again in his mind the sudden plunge of headlights over the ravine as he forced the jeep down its slippery side and across the raging torrent.

Had she fallen in love with him then, or was it when she had thrust her face into his neck and clung to his re-assuringly broad shoulder as he forded the creek with her in his arms? Or any of the dozen times she had watched for his return from the day's work, noting the creases round eyes and firm mouth made more promi-nent from the layer of sand-like dust powdering his skin?

And did it really matter? He was already committed to someone else, someone who must mean a lot to him if he was prepared to leave this beautiful house of his fathers and live in what she had come to consider a modern monstrosity.

Tomorrow she would go and see it, this shrine to the future mistress of Clearwater. So far, in the short time she had had free between chores, she had done little more than walk curiously round the meticulously maintained ranch buildings, Dusty at her heels, looking longingly at the corralled horses who soon learned to associate her figure with the illicit treats she brought for them. Alex and his brothers appeared to alternate horses, so that on

some days the fierce-looking but magnificent Arab named
Caliph, the mount only Alex rode, paced the outer
perimeter of the corral, impatient for his master's return.
Only on the third occasion of her visits did Caliph deign
to shoulder aside the lesser horses and accept with royal
disdain the goodies Joanna offered.

But now, exhausted emotionally as well as physically,
Joanna decided on an early night. Usually now when
Glen was at home she made up a large-sized sandwich of
cold beef or ham slices, lettuce and tomato, and put it in
the fridge for his late-night snack. However much he ate
at the evening meal, he always contrived to visit the kitchen before bedtime, inventing sandwiches of such re-
volting concoctions that she had begun making them
herself. But tonight she sighed her relief at his absence.

A long soak in the bath relaxed her limbs, and she
padded barefoot and in her hyacinth blue lace-edged
nightdress back to the bedroom. Discovering that it was
still earlier than the hour that would bring sleep, she
reached into the large closet opposite her bed for a warm
robe.

Her nostrils pricked at the unfamiliar odour that met
them ... unfamiliar, yet bearing a haunting memory of
hay-scented stables, of animal life. Her eyes dropped to
the floor, and she stifled the scream that rose to her
throat as a black mass moved at her feet.

Horrified, she stared down at a complacent Dusty and
the six fat black pups who squealed and squirmed and
reached greedily to nurse from their mother.

# CHAPTER SIX

'ANNA? Anna, are you asleep yet?'

Slowly Joanna's eyes lifted to the door when Alex knocked yet another time.

'No ... no, I'm not,' she said in a strangled voice, and barely waited to see the handle turn and the door begin to open before she returned her attention to Dusty and her family in the closet.

'I forgot to give you this cheque. You can come into town with me tomorrow and—— Good God, what's going on in here?'

Joanna turned luminously tender eyes up to him, mindless of her revealing nightdress, before dropping to her knees.

'Oh, Alex, look! Six beautiful babies, can you believe it?'

'I can believe it all right,' he returned in a grim voice, his eyes growing flint-like as they went down to the new family. 'What I can't believe is that you would bring Dusty into the house when I'd expressly told you to keep her outside!'

'What?' Joanna glanced bemusedly up at him, then looked back at the dog and her little ones, her mouth curving into a smile when Dusty magnanimously allowed her to lift one of the puppies into her arms. 'Look, Alex, isn't he lovely? He's so fat, just like a butterball!'

'No doubt from all the extra feeding you've given his mother,' Alex retorted drily, and it was only then that his anger seeped through to Joanna's consciousness.

The puppy mewling in her arms, she turned to face Alex incredulously. 'Alex, you can't be that hard-hearted! This is the miracle of new life, doesn't it do anything for you?'

'Not half as much as it's going to do for you when they keep you awake all night with their crying! You know they can't be moved out of here for a few days?'

'I don't mind. Human babies cry, but their parents don't throw them out of the house because of it.'

After a moment of his silence she turned to look up at him and surprised an odd expression in his eyes. Then it was gone, and he said tightlipped: 'There are other bedrooms you can sleep in for the time the pups have to be in here.'

'No!' Joanna watched in horror as he began to take her clothes from the closet. 'What are you doing?'

'Moving your things into the boot room. I don't care to have my—*housekeeper*—smelling of dogs!'

When he stalked out with a large armful of clothes, Joanna bent and returned the wriggling pup to his mother, straightening as Alex returned and ruthlessly tackled the remainder of her clothes, waiting until he came back into the room before speaking.

'I really didn't know Dusty was in here,' she said quietly. 'She must have slipped in today when the porch door was open. I kept going out to see if she was there ...'

'To feed her?'

'Yes,' she confessed humbly, then rallied to justify herself. 'But she hasn't been allowed in the house since you put her out.'

'She's a *working* dog, Anna, not a house pet.'

'And you make no exception for—for pregnancy and motherhood, is that it?'

'Can't you understand? Once she's used to the house, she'll be useless as a work dog.'

'And that's all that matters to you, isn't it?' Joanna cried. 'Everybody has to work to utmost capacity—the animals, your brothers, your housekeeper—everybody!'

'Including myself,' he added tautly. 'That's what our life is all about. If I ease up, everybody else eases up all along the line. And a working ranch can't afford that kind of leisure.'

Suddenly Joanna wanted to cry, to hold him in her arms and comfort the Alex she had glimpsed momentarily, the man who had had too many responsibilities too soon. But all she could get out was a choked:

'I'm sorry, Alex. I shouldn't have said what I did.'

'It's all right.' He gave a twisted smile. 'I'm used to that kind of thinking. Most of the time, Glen looks on me as some kind of tyrant.'

'Alex, he doesn't,' Joanna denied fiercely, then turned her head slightly away from him before going on hesitantly about a matter that was none of her concern. 'He—he admires you a lot, but ... well, you're not the most tolerant man on earth, are you?'

His tone was lightly amused. 'I thought I'd been very tolerant where *you're* concerned, considering your gross inexperience for the job you undertook to do here.'

'I—yes, you have been,' she conceded, going on hurriedly: 'But we're talking about Glen.'

'Glen's been complaining to you about my behaviour?' The amusement had disappeared under a layer of ice.

'No, of course not! I—I just can't help noticing that you come down pretty hard on him sometimes, for very little reason.' She tilted her head at him defiantly. 'I think you forget that he's twenty years old, a young man with a right to decide things for himself.'

'Such as?'

She shrugged. 'Where he'll go in his free time, where he spends it, what time he gets home ... they're all things that most young men decide for themselves.'

'Maybe Glen isn't like most young men,' Alex retorted drily, turning to leave when Joanna's next words halted him and sent his head round in an angry swivel towards her.

'Did your father keep you on the same kind of tight rein?'

'He didn't have to,' he said shortly, eyes like gimlets.

'And I don't think you have to keep a foot on the back of Glen's neck all the time!' she declared hotly, flushing when his glance flicked contemptuously over her.

'You wouldn't. Fortunately for Glen, that's not your province. In future, confine yourself to your so-called household arts!'

The door had slammed behind him before Joanna had a chance to even close her mouth, which had parted in astonished hurt. She had told Alex that he wasn't the most tolerant person in the world, but that hadn't been strictly true until his last tightlipped remark.

Too late she recognised how truly tolerant he had been in view of her obvious lack of the skills he had employed her to practise. Another man would have sent her packing as soon as the washed-out bridge was recrossable.

Ignoring the constant soft mewlings of the pups, she arranged the bed pillows behind her and sat on top of the bedcovers, her brow wrinkled in thought. Why *hadn't* Alex sent her away after that first evening at Clearwater, when he had probed her background and obviously come to the conclusion that she wasn't what she said she was?

Especially when he had thought, right from the beginning, that she was yet another marriage hopeful despatched from the city by his sister Liz.

Thinking about Liz brought the carroty hair and freckled face to mind, and Joanna went over again the conversations she had had with Alex's sister. Had there been the slightest indication that Liz had in mind for her a role far more encompassing than housekeeper at Clearwater?

No, she was sure not. Yet Liz had made no effort to hide her antipathy to the girl she believed her eldest brother would marry. From words let drop in her hearing, Joanna knew that all of the younger Harpers felt the same way about Paula Erikson. Perhaps because of her swift breaking of her engagement to Alex upon discovering the extent of his responsibilities towards them. Responsibilities which Alex, being Alex, wouldn't think twice about assuming.

And that brought her back to the reason why he had kept her on in face of her obvious unsuitability for the job. He must have believed implicitly the part of her story about an unemployed father who worked in a factory.

Joanna swallowed a lump of guilt in her throat. What would Alex do if he found out the truth about her background? After his caustic suggestion that she stick to her household chores instead of interfering with the Harpers' personal lives, she could well imagine his towering rage at being deceived into a show of softheartedness. What had Liz said? Something about not letting Alex find out about the deception, that he couldn't stand dishonesty.

Until now, Joanna hadn't been able to either. But what about Alex himself? His behaviour in making love to her while more or less engaged to another girl was far from ethical, but maybe in this land of rough he-men ethics went out the window where women were concerned. Perhaps he regarded her as fair game especially when, she blushed to remember, she had responded so freely to his kisses.

Whatever his motives had been, Joanna was honest enough to appraise her own and to come up with the staggering possibility that she was falling in love with Alex Harper. And that would never do, not in a million years.

Joanna knew instinctively that it was much later than usual when she awoke the next morning. The room was quite bright despite the closely woven curtains drawn over the windows, and she blinked at the relentlessly ticking alarm clock on the bedside table.

Ten o'clock! She must have slept through the ringing of the alarm—but when her fingers groped to the button she found it pressed down to the 'off' position.

Squeals from the closet reminded her forcibly of the pups and the hours of sleep they had cost her during the night. Throwing back the covers, she slid from the bed and went barefoot to the closet, her stunned eyes taking in the bowl still containing milk near Dusty's head, the other dish that had obviously held meat of some kind.

Her eyes went slowly from the dishes beside the dog to the alarm clock on the night table. It must have been Alex who had come into the room, who had brought food and drink for the dog, turned off the alarm so that she herself could sleep on.

In the distance she heard the phone ring once ... twice ... then its abrupt cutting off. By the time she had drawn back the curtains, blinking in the sunlight that flooded the room, booted feet clipped across the hall and through the kitchen, the sound ceasing with the muted bang of the back door.

When at last she reached the kitchen, showered and dressed in deep purple slacks and lilac-coloured loose shirt, Joanna saw that Alex had already eaten the breakfast he must have cooked for himself and stacked the dishes untidily on the counter. Coffee was keeping warm in the percolator, and she sipped gratefully at the fragrant brew before tossing two slices of bread into the toaster.

Again she reflected on what a strange man Alex Harper was, unlike any other she had ever known. After his tightlipped anger of the night before, she had half expected to find herself bundled off on the next bus to Vancouver, yet he had guessed about her sleepless night and thoughtfully turned off the alarm. He had exploded in wrath over Dusty's presence in her closet, but he had gone to the trouble of carrying in sustenance to the animal.

A strange man ... and one it had been easy for her to lose her head over. How lucky Paula Erikson was, she thought with an unconscious sigh as she buttered her toast and poured another coffee, standing at the counter to eat and drink, staring sightlessly from the window.

So far, she hadn't let herself think too much about the kisses he had given and extracted from her. They had obviously meant little to him, his recovery had been so rapid after them, mocking amusement quickly replacing any passion he might have felt. And that had acted like a dam on her own emotional reaction, but now ...

She deliberately let herself remember the touch of his mouth on hers, the firm mould of his lips teasing lightly but sensually over her own sensitive surfaces, promising yet unfulfilling. The sure, confident caress of his hands had spoken of practised ease with a woman, and she guessed that Paula had been far from the only female in his life, despite his premature family responsibilities.

Pulling herself together with a mental shake, she decided that her first action in her late starting day should be a walk to clear away the cobwebs.

If only it could be a gallop over the hills on one of Alex's horses, she mourned, catching a glimpse of them spread out in the lushy green paddock on the far side of the stables. Maybe one day, when the Harper brothers were away and none of the hired hands was around— but then Alex never left the ranch without at least one man to see to things, so she might as well forget that.

She knew in which direction the new house lay, having seen its bulk softened by the trees surrounding it and heard the sounds of construction men at work. It was a bare quarter-mile walk south of the ranch, and Joanna noted as she drew near that the house had been cleverly sited at the head of a spreading valley of eye-catching beauty. Colours contrasted and blended in endless array from the delicate green of newly unfurled aspen trees amid dark green spruce to the purple-smudged mountains in the far distance.

The house of red cedar looked serviceably attractive at its entrance side, but she realised when she had picked her way over lumber scraps and woodshavings that the main rooms would face the grandeur of the valley beyond.

It was ultra-modern, with soaring windows and an as yet unrailed gallery floor above the large hall-living room area. And everywhere there was the sweet yet pungent scent of cedar. The theme of the house seemed to be a light and bright airiness which Joanna was sure would appeal to many people, though her own tastes lay in different directions.

'You're beautiful,' she spoke aloud to the house, hands on trim hips as she stood before the living room windows, 'but I really prefer the old place.'

'Do you?'

Joanna jumped visibly as the voice came from behind and to her right. Whirling, her shoes scattering a flurry of shavings, she stared open-mouthed at Alex, who was leaning nonchalantly against one of the upright support posts.

'What do you mean by creeping up on me like that?' she spluttered. 'I could have had a heart attack!'

'You haven't reached the age for heart attacks yet,' he observed mildly, detaching himself from the post and coming lazily towards her, his boots sounding hollow on the bare wood floor. 'And it was you who crept up on me!'

'You could have let me know you were there,' Joanna grumbled less abrasively, taking note, now that her heart had stilled to a steadier rhythm, that he looked more attractive than ever in yellow knit sports shirt and corded pants the colour of oatmeal. The shirt clung where it touched his muscled torso and exposed the tensile strength of brown arms below its short sleeves.

'How was I to know you weren't a prowler, a thief out to take what you could find?'

'Like what?' she scorned, glancing round the bare room. 'Woodshavings to add to my collection?'

His mouth curved slightly in a smile, but he made no reply to that, instead turning to stand with his shoulder next to hers to gaze out to the valley view.

'So you don't like the house?' he asked softly without looking at her.

'I didn't say that,' Joanna muttered uncomfortably, twisting her head round to look frowningly up at him.

She wished he hadn't come to stand so close to her so that whatever it was that many males exuded flooded her senses and made them waver. 'I did say it was beautiful.'

'But you prefer the old place.'

Now she was wishing that he had kept his eyes ahead, because they were looking down oddly into hers, so close that she could see the paler flecks amongst the brown.

As with a great physical effort, she pulled her own gaze away and moved slightly aside, separating them physically although she still felt the tug of something else between them. Forcing what she hoped was a casual shrug, she said :

'I doesn't matter what I think, does it?'

'It might.'

'Why? Surely it's only important to you what your— your bride thinks of it.'

'One woman's opinion is pretty much the same as any,' he returned carelessly.

Joanna drew breath noisily. 'If that isn't the most arrogant thing I ever heard! For your information, I wouldn't want the house for myself, but no doubt Paula has her *own* opinion!'

His only answer was a satisfied smile, and she realised he had trapped her in some way she wasn't aware of.

Then : 'Paula hasn't seen this place yet,' he said in a conversational tone, and Joanna stared up at him blankly.

'Oh, I guess it's—to be a surprise for her.' An uncomfortable stone seemed to have lodged in her chest.

'It's to be a surprise, yes.'

'Don't you think you should have consulted her first? It's a big undertaking on an offchance.'

Alex shrugged, thumbs hooked easily into the silver-buckled belt at his waist. 'Taste is pretty easy to determine when you know a person well.'

'I—I suppose so.' Joanna turned away. 'Well, I have to get back to the house. I—I want to do some baking.'

'Oh?' His tone was thoughtful, but seemed level enough as he fell into step beside her, taking her arm to help her round the wooden trestles scattered across the floor. 'I'm sorry about our trip into town. I'd intended to leave early and take you to lunch, but you didn't seem up to it when I checked on the pups this morning.'

A quick glance at his face as they emerged into the sunlight told Joanna that, if the gleam in his eye was anything to go by, he had checked her sleeping self more intently than the pups. The thought brought a wave of colour under her skin, and he mocked softly:

'Don't worry, you don't snore a lot.'

'I don't snore at all!' she whipped back indignantly, seeing from his grin that he had been baiting her again.

'Only your husband will ever know for sure.'

Joanna managed a scornful laugh. 'In this day and age? You really do live in the back of beyond, don't you?'

She was unprepared for the immediate frown that sliced down between his brows. 'That reminds me of something I wanted to talk to you about,' he said tersely, taking her arm and urging her to the far side of the house. 'You can ride back with me on Caliph.'

'No!' Joanna drew her arm away from his confining hand and dug her heels into the dusty earth.

'You're afraid of horses?'

'No.'

'Then you're afraid of me.' One bronzed hand came out to lift her chin, opening her face to his faintly amused scrutiny. 'It's been years since I ravished a girl on horseback within a quarter of a mile of the ranch.'

'You flatter yourself,' Joanna said stonily, and marched over to where Caliph cropped the succulent grass beside the house, remembering just in time that she was supposed to be a novice and not expected to know what a horse was all about.

Alex swung himself into the Western saddle first, making Joanna's teeth grit together when he explained with infuriating patience just where she should place which foot to join him there. So irritated was she that the leg she swung up and over the saddle caught on the high pommel and she felt herself slide off to the side until hard hands lifted her effortlessly and settled her firmly on the tooled leather. At least she had confirmed in his mind that she was a non-rider, she thought sourly.

'There, isn't this cosy?' a voice mocked uncomfortably close to her ear, and her spine stiffened away from the hard male torso behind her. But she could do nothing about the arm that cradled her ribs as the other reached round her to the reins.

'I thought you wanted to talk,' she tosed back frigidly as Caliph began to move under them.

'I do,' Alex assured her, holding the reins loosely in one hand, the arm round her midriff tightening to pull her back against him. 'It's much better if you relax, though.'

Knowing the truth of this, Joanna allowed herself to lean slightly into him, and said crisply: 'All right, what is it?'

'I want you to tell me about Liz.'

'Liz?'

'Have you met this—Phil she's been seeing?'

Joanna stared straight ahead at the ranch buildings in the distance. 'Once,' she said briefly.

'What kind of fellow is he?'

Her shoulders lifted in a slight shrug. 'How would I know, on the strength of one meeting? He seemed—clean-cut, reasonably prosperous, fond of Liz.'

'How close are they?'

'If you're asking whether they live together, I wouldn't know,' she said flatly. 'I don't think so, but even if they do, it's nobody's business but their own, is it? Liz is twenty-four, old enough to know what she's doing.'

Surprisingly, she felt a rough chin rub thoughfully on the silken skeins of her hair.

'You think I'm wrong to worry about my sister's happiness?' he asked gruffly.

'Of course not.' Joanna blinked away unexpected tears and in defence added flippantly: 'Once you have a wife and children of your own to worry about, you won't be so concerned with your brothers and sister.'

She felt his hand lift and strong fingers came round to turn her face up to his. 'You could be right,' he said softly. 'You could also become a pretty good rider.'

'How would you know at this speed?' she mocked, trembling as he released her chin. He had been about to kiss her, she knew; what she wasn't so sure about was her own surge of longing to feel his mouth against hers, this time with no holds barred. But somebody had to think of Paula, even if it wasn't her prospective husband.

'You want to go faster?'

'Why not?'

At least that way they would reach the ranch quicker, and she could escape from this too intimate contact with him. But Caliph, presumably at a touch from his master, veered off to the left and broke into a trot.

'Okay?' Alex breathed at her ear.

'Fine.'

Already Joanna was feeling the accustomed thrill of

excitement as the animal moved under her, sensed
Caliph's impatience at the curbing of his powerful
muscles, an impatience that matched her own urge to fly
with the wind.

Then they were flying, it seemed, Caliph's stride
lengthening as Alex gave him his head. Joanna's black
hair, freed from the confines of the white scarf tying it
neatly back, whipped behind her in the wind that took
her breath and made her lean forward on the steely arm
that still held her.

The hills she had longed to ride over passed under the
sure-footed Caliph, and mixed in the wind were the
scents of early clover and new grass and moist rich earth.
Nothing could be nearer to heaven for Joanna, and she
felt a sharp tug of disappointment when she lifted her
head as the Arab slowed and she saw that they had returned in a semi-circle to the ranch.

'Oh, Alex, that was great!' She twisted her head round
to smile uninhibitedly up at him, her cheeks whipped to
a glowing pink. 'Thank you.'

Alex brushed away a few strands of her hair from his
face before answering, a puzzled frown creasing his
brows. 'You're sure you've never ridden before?'

Sudden caution stemmed her smile and her eyes dropped to the level of his mouth as she said gaily: 'Was I
that good, that you have to ask?'

'I'd say you were very good. You have a natural seat
on a horse, and I think you'd make a fine horsewoman.'

'Hardly that, Alex,' a woman's drawl came from beside them, 'if you have to sit behind her and hold her
on!'

Startled, Joanna realised that Caliph had stopped moving and that they were stationed by the corral gate. Her
head swivelled in the direction of the voice, and she was

unaware of her automatic movement backwards to lean against Alex's stalwart body, only aware of gratefulness for the hard arm around her.

The woman who had spoken so caustically came towards them from the corral fence opposite, the cool symmetry of her tall blonde-topped figure belied by the blazing red of her pants suit. Pale blue eyes looked up at them from a face of chiselled perfection. Slender nose of sculptured beauty, mouth that must at times be fuller than its present tightlipped state.

'You're early, Paula,' Alex's voice rumbled against Joanna's back, and she felt deprived when his warm body lifted away from her as he swung himself lithely to the ground.

'I got through quicker than I thought,' Paula's voice softened when she spoke solely to Alex. 'When I called you, Dad was still arguing with Jack Flint.'

So the phone call this morning had been from her, Joanna thought dully, feeling an inexplicable urge to spur Caliph into action once more and disappear from the sight of these two beautiful beings seemingly oblivious of her presence.

But Alex remembered her at that moment, and reached up to clasp her waist with both hands as she slid from the horse.

Keeping one arm around Joanna, Alex introduced the two girls—an introduction Paula acknowledged with the frosty air of a duchess being introduced to her kitchen-maid.

'She's very young to be a housekeeper, isn't she?' she directed to Alex as if Joanna wasn't there.

'She's doing just fine,' Alex surprisingly defended her. 'In fact, she's about to do some baking, which should be ready just about the time we get back from wherever it is you want me to take you.'

'I told you, sweetie,' Paula sent back with barely veiled chagrin, 'the auction at the Jephson place.'

'Oh, yes. Poor old Jephson.' Alex sighed. 'Too bad he has to sell out after forty-odd years of hard work.'

'He's a fool, and always has been,' the blonde girl replied curtly. 'If he'd played his cards right, he could have had a valuable property there.'

'I don't suppose he cared too much about property values after his wife left him,' Alex retorted evenly.

'And why did she do that?' Paula demanded, turning her back on Joanna. 'Because he had no get up and go, that's why! No woman can be happy married to a man without ambition to better himself.'

'If you'll excuse me,' Joanna inserted in the ensuing pause, 'I have work to do.'

Neither of the beautiful people seemed to notice her departure, and she fumed as she walked back to the house. How could Alex even think of being engaged to such a woman, let alone build a modern edifice for them to live in after their marriage?

All Joanna's sympathies were with the unknown Jephson, who had seemingly earned such scathing remarks from Paula. Maybe his wife had been the same type as Paula, she thought irritably as she banged into the house. How could Alex be so concerned for his sister's happiness, and so blind to his own?

But perhaps Paula's was the kind of personality he needed to match his own, she pondered as she reached for the cookbook lovingly inscribed by his mother. What would Anne Harper have thought of her beloved first-born marrying a woman like Paula? Joanna's finger creased open the page marked 'Alex's favourite' but the writing blurred before her eyes.

Alex and Paula had been engaged at the time of his parents' death, so they must have known Paula ... perhaps liked her. Or had they forced themselves to like her because she was their son's choice as a wife?

Sighing exasperatedly at her own fanciful thoughts, Joanna concentrated on the lovingly constructed recipe.

# CHAPTER SEVEN

THE kitchen was still filled with the spicy aroma of Alex's fruit slices when he and Paula finally returned from the auction. His head lifted as he came into the kitchen alone, his nose taking in the aroma like a pointer hot on the chase.

'What's that?' he asked.

'You'll find out when I serve it,' Joanna returned shortly, despondent at the thought that she sounded like the irascible cooks she had read about in ancient novels. 'Do you prefer tea or coffee?'

'Tea, I guess. We're out on the porch.'

'I'll bring it.'

Paula seemed in no better mood than her own when Joanna took the laden tray out to the broad front veranda, but she rallied as Joanna set delicate china before each of them.

'I was really looking forward to the Shakespeare weekend,' she said, filled with gloom. 'It's really too bad of them to cancel out at the last minute just because of some stupid Festival in Seattle.'

'Why don't you put on your own Shakespeare show?' Alex asked, amused.

Paula glared at his lazily smiling eyes. 'Don't be ridiculous,' she snapped. 'It wouldn't be much of a problem for me to learn lines, but where would I find anyone else around here capable of learning Shakespearian English?'

'Oh, I don't know.' His eyes lifted idly to Joanna as she lifted the tray from the table. 'Anna here has aspirations towards acting, and'—his eyes roved over her black hair and slight figure—'I can just see her as Juliet.'

Paula's eyes cut Joanna to ribbons. 'She might look the part, but that's a long way from being able to remember lines of prose and deliver them effectively.'

An imp of mischief sparked by anger prompted Joanna's: 'You mean something like—

"The quality of mercy is not strain'd,
It droppeth as the gentle rain from heaven
Upon the place beneath: it is twice bless'd;
It blesseth him that gives and him that takes:"'

Oh, why couldn't she have remembered these words as well when she had been given the part of Portia? They flowed free and clear into her mouth now.

'"But mercy is above this sceptred sway,
It is enthroned in the heart of kings,
It is an attribute to God himself ..."'

'Very pretty,' Paula sneered, the first to recover from her surprise. Alex still stared at Joanna with a stunned look.

'You're very young to have studied Shakespeare as well as learning how to keep house.'

'I did go to school,' Joanna replied sweetly, and whipped off the white cloth covering the fruit slices, seeing Alex's slow frown as the glazed brown pastries caught his eye.

'These look like——' he exclaimed, reaching out a tanned hand to take one of the slices and biting into it with his strong white teeth. 'They are!' He looked up again at Joanna questioningly. 'I haven't tasted these since my mother used to make them for me.'

Joanna coloured slightly. 'I found the recipe in her cookbook ... she'd marked it as your favourite.'

Alex looked fixedly at the pastries for a long moment,

then said emotionally: 'Thank you, Anna. I appreciate it.'

'How sweet of you to make them especially for us, Anna,' Paula interjected smoothly, and to Alex: 'You were right, darling, she really is a treasure. It's so hard to get help these days, you should really hold on to Anna here.'

'I mean to.'

'If—if you need anything more, I'm in the kitchen,' Joanna stammered hurriedly, thankful to escape from Alex's painfully penetrating look.

How easy it was, she thought as she sank gratefully into a kitchen chair and sipped on the coffee she preferred to tea, to save a man from a fate that was, in her opinion, worse than death! All she had to do was to make something that evoked the emotional overtones of a mother who had loved him.

Not that she expected anything permanent to grow between them from the mere making of a few fruit slices, she reminded herself hastily, but she was now firmly on the side of Liz, Nick and Glen in their antipathy towards Paula as a sister-in-law. Alex had his faults, to be sure, but none that added up to a life sentence married to a woman like Paula.

That opinion was reinforced not long after by the appearance of Paula in the kitchen, the pale blue of her eyes darting around as if hopeful of finding something to fault.

'I came to tell you—er—*Anna*,' she emphasised with a cool precision that made mockery of the warm tones of her pants suit, 'that Mr Harper will be out to dinner tonight. So perhaps you'd like to entertain a—friend?'

'Friend?'

'Oh, come on now,' the older girl said with sickening

coyness, 'I'm sure a pretty girl like you has made lots of friends even in the short time you've been here.'

'Only Alex, Nick, Glen and Nick's fiancée, Shirley,' Joanna returned blankly.

Paula gave a deprecating laugh. 'Oh, well, you can hardly class them as *friends*, can you?' She hesitated prettily before going on: 'I wouldn't read too much into Alex taking you riding with him this morning if I were you. His softheartedness carries him away at times.'

'Like the time when his parents died and he took on the raising of his brothers and sister?' Joanna asked innocently, rewarded by the frown that spoiled the symmetry of Paula's features.

The other girl was saved a reply when Alex came into the kitchen, looking so different in charcoal lounge suit and immaculate white shirt that Joanna stared speechlessly at him. His dress had been much more casual the previous Saturday, so she presumed that he was taking Paula to a more exclusive place for dinner.

'Ready?'

'Yes,' Paula replied, smiling as she went to his side. 'My, don't you look grand! I'm going to have my work cut out to make myself presentable enough for you!'

She could say that again, Joanna thought sourly, gratified when Alex said a trifle impatiently:

'As long as you don't take for ever doing it. You told the others seven o'clock, didn't you?'

'Yes, but they'll have a drink or two to pass the time if we're not there.'

'Hmm.' Alex turned back from the door as they were about to leave, saying to Joanna: 'I guess you know I won't be eating at home tonight.' At her nod, his eyes narrowed speculatively on her. 'What are you doing tonight, Anna?'

'Me? Oh, I have p-plenty to keep me occupied. There's some ironing to finish, and the pups to see to.'

'Pups?' Paula queried with a distasteful quirk on her pursed mouth.

'Dusty decided to have her youngsters in Anna's room,' Alex explained, a faint smile curving his mouth. He turned thoughtfully back to Joanna. 'You haven't had any real time off since you came. Why don't you come out to dinner with us? I doubt if you'll cook much for yourself.'

'Oh, Alex!' Paula expostulated, while Joanna thought guiltily about the sandwich she was contemplating making for herself. 'I know you mean to be kind, but she'd feel so uncomfortable as the odd woman out.'

Alex's brows rose as he surveyed Paula coolly. 'I hadn't realised it was a pairing off affair. I thought it was a celebration dinner for your brother's birthday. You've asked two or three of his unattached friends, haven't you?'

'Yes, but——' Paula hesitated and glanced over at Joanna with a pained frown. 'Alex, honey, you're just embarrassing the girl. I don't suppose she has anything suitable to wear, for one thing.'

Joanna, far from feeling embarrassment, was beginning to enjoy the exchange between them. Paula, apart from being a snob, was far less sure of herself regarding Alex than she would like to believe.

'You seemed to have plenty of clothes when I moved them from your room last night,' Alex addressed Joanna, and looked round impatiently when Paula asked frigidly:

'When you did what?'

'I had to move her clothes out or she'd have smelled of dog for evermore,' he said inelegantly, and turned back to say briskly to Joanna: 'Well? Have you something suitable to wear for dinner and dancing?'

Ignoring the flinty cast of Paula's eye, Joanna said demurely: 'Yes, I have. But I do have to see to the pups.'

'I'll see to them while you get changed,' he dismissed that problem, and the one posed by a scowling Paula. 'Help yourself to a drink. We shouldn't be long. For a female, Anna gets dressed pretty fast.'

'Does she now!' Paula's lips were tautened to thinness as she turned away to the door, and before sweeping through it she managed to throw Joanna a malignant look that told the younger girl all she wanted to know.

She would go with them, do everything in her power to drive the wedge deeper between them. Acting had proved to be one of the big failures in her life, she thought as she sped to the boot room, but with only Alex as her audience, she should be able to carry off her little charade. It shouldn't be too difficult, she reflected wistfully, selecting from the rack the only extravagant item she had allowed herself to bring. And she hadn't expected to wear the swirling froth of short flame chiffon dress; most of the clothes she had packed to come to Clearwater had been the plainest, most serviceable gear she possessed. This one indulgence had at the time been a half-conscious defence against the unknown in alien country.

By the time she had showered quickly and returned to her bedroom, Alex had already attended to Dusty. It took her only a few minutes more to dress and apply some deft touches of make-up, then to brush the silk glossiness of her hair until it gleamed with blue-black lights. She was just casting a rueful look at her hands, where the nails had lost their perfect ovals and were uneven in length—housework was hard on them—when

Alex knocked lightly and came in.

Joanna whirled round, the sudden swift beat of her heart against her ribs telling her that she hadn't dressed in her finery solely to sever Paula's hold on him.

The stunned amazement in his brown eyes as they went slowly over her was more than gratifying, but as they returned to her face and cloud of shining hair around it, his mouth inexplicably tightened and his eyes grew cool, freezing the tentative smile hovering at her lips.

'How—how do I look?'

'Fine,' he replied noncommittally, his eyes lighting on the hand she had raised instinctively to her throat. 'Except that your nails are a mess.'

'I—I know,' she stammered, hurt by his indifference. Surely her mirror hadn't lied to that extent! 'There isn't time to do anything about them.'

He turned and went towards the closet. 'You have ten minutes while I exercise Dusty.'

Joanna wasted two of her precious minutes blinking back the stinging tears that filled her eyes. Then her head came up in an angry arc and she reached for a file from the dressing table behind her. Trimming the nails with swift, sure strokes, she reflected bitterly that Alex deserved Paula for a wife ... their vile natures matched perfectly! Though she had to admit, as she brushed on colour that matched her dress, that Alex had a dual nature, to say the least.

It must have been kindness on his part to ask her out to dinner, especially in face of Paula's unmistakable opposition, but he had been quick to negate that kindness with his chilling appraisal of her appearance. Perhaps he shared that streak of snobbishness with Paula and resented his housekeeper emerging as a swan from the kitchen.

Waving her hands about to dry the polish, Joanna tightened her lips and made a vow that, somehow or other, she would teach Alex a lesson that night. There were to be unattached men at the party, he had said, and surely there would be at least one who would not object to dancing with a housekeeper!

She would show Alex Harper that his opinion didn't matter a hoot to her. It might even be fun to flirt a little with a man who had no idea that she was James Thomas's daughter. At least she would know that he liked her for herself, and not for her father's wealth.

The evening couldn't have been more of a success if Joanna had planned it for months, instead of in a few furious minutes while caring for her nails. Which, she thought with a sense of complacency as she glanced at her left hand spread on a broad male shoulder, looked quite good in their shorter state.

Since their first moments at the fairly new Cariboo Roadhouse south of town, Joanna hadn't lacked for partners both for the dinner and the dancing afterwards. Peter Erikson, Paula's brother, proved to be a big, bluff edition of Paula, with similar thick blond hair and pale blue eyes. But there the resemblance ended. Peter's nature seemed as uncomplicated as Paula's was intricate, though his heavy Nordic frame concealed a witty intelligence which intrigued Joanna and made her understand why he and Alex had been friends since childhood.

Joanna had met Peter while she and Alex waited an interminable time for Paula to emerge from her dressing at the beautifully set Erikson home. Clear-cut lines de-

lineated the white frame two-storied structure, and the
living room where they waited was coolly functional in
Scandinavian style. But it suited the Eriksons, Joanna
decided after being introduced to the parents, who had
evidently bestowed their blue eyes and fair hair liberally
on their offspring.

When Paula at last appeared, soignée in a navy silk
dress which clung to the lines of her tall figure, Joanna
wondered that such wholesomely simple people had produced such a daughter. Alex couldn't be blamed for, in
the first place, becoming engaged to marry her or, in the
present, being in the process of building a house for her.
She was a woman any man would be proud to be seen
with, proud to own as his ... wife.

Yet her brother seemed casual about their relationship. 'Sometimes I wish that Paula and Alex would make
a pair,' he remarked as he held Joanna a little too closely
while they danced, 'but then I wonder if it would be a
good thing. Paula likes her own way in most things, but
Alex isn't exactly the type to give in to a woman on any
count, so ...'

'So why don't we just leave it to them?' Joanna suggested tartly, loosening the hold between them and looking miserably over to where Paula and Alex, alone at
the long table, talked seriously together.

If Alex was in love with her, Joanna, would she be
content with serious conversation at a party table? No,
she answered her own question without hesitation. She
would want to dance with him, be held by him, to know
that he desired her as much as she ... desired him.

The realisation that she did desire Alex made Joanna's
spine stiffen in instinctive denial. That was what he expected. Liz, his sister, had prepared him for girls anxious
to know him better. Girls who had impinged lightly on

the quiet life of Clearwater, then faded into oblivion. Just as she, Joanna, would fade into obscurity when the regular housekeeper returned to take up her duties.

'What did you say?' she asked Peter, who stared down at her with half-amused belligerence.

'I said,' he whispered at her ear, 'why are we bothering about Paula and Alex? They're happy enough together ... and I could be very happy with someone like you, Anna.'

Laughter gurgled up in her throat. 'How many girls have you said that to in the past year or so?'

'Not many. And none of them like you.' He smiled down into her face. 'You've made a hit with all the men here tonight, you know. Me most of all. Can I see you again, Anna?'

'Why not?' she returned lightly as the dance ended. 'You know where I live.'

His eyes took on a wary look as he led her, arm around her waist, back to the table where Alex and Paula had seemingly finished their conversation. The tight line of Alex's jaw as he glanced up, first at Peter and then flickeringly over Joanna, indicated that the conversation had not been as satisfactory as he had hoped. Paula, too, had a frosty look about her light blue eyes when they lit on her brother's arm round Joanna's petite waist.

No sooner had Peter settled Joanna in her place at the table than Chris Lazen, a man little older than herself whom she had danced with several times, appeared at her side, his darkly handsome face cajoling her to dance with him again. About to accept, Joanna shut her mouth suddenly when Alex spoke from across the table.

'As I brought Anna, and this has to be the last dance for us, I'm claiming it,' he clipped, rising and coming round the table to where Joanna sat in troubled bewilderment.

He had danced with several of the girls attending the party, and with Paula once or twice, but had shown no interest until now in dancing with herself. His strong grip on her arm left no room for refusal, and she rose, giving Chris a regretful smile and catching the venomous frown Paula threw her way as Alex led her to the small dance floor.

She looked thoughtfully up at the hard chin and firmly held mouth above her head as Alex took her into his arms and they began to move to the slow throb of music. Had he asked her to dance as a way of repaying Paula for her stubbornness over whatever they had been discussing? It must be something like that, she decided, when they came round the floor towards the birthday table and Alex's rigid posture melted suddenly and the arm circling her waist tightened to pull her closer to the intimidating bigness of his body. Amazed at first when she felt the hard chin against her head, a wry smile pulled at her mouth when, circling in his arms, she met Paula's frigid stare again.

Some imp of mischief slid her hand along the broad shoulder until it reached the back of Alex's neck, where her fingers stroked seductively against the short wiry hairs until he jerked his head up with a sharply indrawn breath and stared coolly down into her pseudo-innocent gaze.

'I see now why you've been so popular tonight,' he said harshly, manoeuvring her between two other couples on the dimly lit floor.

'I'm not sure what you mean,' she murmured faintly ... and faint she was feeling with the heady sensation of how neatly their steps coincided, how firmly the hand at her back guided her. Then reality doused her like a shower of cold water. Paula's steps had fitted his just as well, just as competently. All it meant was that Alex was a good dancer, able to adapt himself to whichever woman he was dancing with.

'Aren't you?' he scoffed softly. 'You're either lying, or a lot more innocent than I can force myself to accept.'

Sarcastically, Joanna bit off: 'Don't strain yourself on my account! It's a matter of supreme indifference as far as I'm concerned. And I don't lie!'

That was no more than the truth, she consoled herself as she stared up at him with flaring nostrils. She hadn't told him an outright untruth since her arrival at Clearwater. It was up to him to interpret her statements as he saw fit.

'Don't you?' His head swooped down until his mouth reached her ear, and he said deliberately: 'Why don't you admit that you've been lying through your teeth since the minute you agreed to come out here?'

'I have not!' she denied indignantly, resenting suddenly the evocative touch of his slowly moving lips against hers, the rigidly held line of his shoulders. 'Show me one instance where I've——'

But the dance ended then, and in the subsequent flurry of their departure there was no more opportunity of private conversation between them. Only a vague impression of Paula's firm-mouthed displeasure remained with her as she compliantly allowed Alex to seat her in the passenger seat of the sleek sports car he had driven to the birthday celebration.

'Isn't Paula coming too?' she asked faintly when Alex got behind the wheel and turned the key in the ignition.

'She's going home with Peter,' he said abruptly, backing and then accelerating the car until the wheels screamed on the tarmac as they shot away from the club.

'Must you drive so fast?' Joanna enquired frigidly when the car swayed giddily at a corner before straightening out.

'Scared?' he jeered, his competent brown hands firm on the wheel.

'No,' she admitted honestly, knowing that she would gladly trust her life to this man. 'I—I just wasn't sure how much you had to drink.'

Alex pulled out on to a straight stretch before replying. 'Less than you, and a lot less than is considered dangerous,' he said then, giving her a sardonic sideways glance. 'That's a lot less than can be said for your behaviour tonight!'

'I don't know what you mean,' she returned primly, focusing her eyes on the rapid flash of jackpines passing the headlights on her right. She was unsure of Alex in this mood. Although she had seen him angry and impatient on previous occasions—most of his ire directed at Glen—there was a cold implacability about him now that sent shivers down her spine.

He laughed softly and without humour. 'I don't believe that, but I'll make myself clearer anyway.' His voice cooled several more degrees. 'You had every unattached man—and one in particular who *is* pretty well attached—hot under the collar tonight.' Sarcastically, he added: 'Around here we're not used to city sexpots levelling their sights on us simple cowboys.'

'I am not—*that*!' Joanna gasped indignantly. 'I'd never even been kissed in a sexy way until I came here and you——' She stopped abruptly and bit furiously on her lip. How he would love that, her admission that his casually given kisses had meant something to her! Obviously the one he had referred to as being 'pretty well attached' was himself, and she wished heartily that her fingers hadn't strayed to his neck while they danced.

'Until I kissed you? Come on now, you don't expect me to believe that!'

'You don't believe much about me, do you?' she asked bitterly, conscious that he had turned into the Clearwater private road.

'No,' he returned with such simple certainty that she gave him a quickly beseeching look before concentrating again on the fenced pastures flipping past in the headlights. Despairingly, she reflected that he had every reason in the world to doubt her. However, she had justified herself earlier, most of what she had told him about herself had been a tissue of lies, or half truths that amount to lies. And Alex wasn't the kind of man who was easily fooled, as his next words proved.

'You're a mystery, Anna Thomas, one I mean to solve before too much time goes by.'

The bleak sense of misery that washed over her took her by surprise. Never in her life had she been as dishonest with anyone as she had been with Alex, a man who, his sister had told her, despised dishonesty. And the irony of it was, she thought as he drew up before the house, that Alex was the last person in the world she wanted to be less than truthful with. She had fallen completely and irrevocably in love with him, regardless of the fact that he was near marriage to another woman.

'Strange,' he said now, his eyes reaching across her to the house, which was lit softly behind the hall windows. 'Nick or Glen must have come back, and I didn't expect either of them. So,' he turned to her in the muted light and slid an arm along the seat behind her shoulders, 'we'll complete our unfinished business out here.'

'B-business?' Joanna stammered. 'Wh-what business?'

She shrank back instinctively when his arm dropped to her shoulders and the warm hardness of his hand on her bare upper arm drew her inexorably back along the seat until her half-turned torso was pressed to his.

'The business you started when we were dancing ... or don't you really know what it does to a man when you run your pretty little fingers through his hair and snuggle up to him like a cuddlesome kitten?'

'I didn't!' she cried, aghast.

'Oh, but you did,' he corrected lazily. His hand came up, warm and compelling, to stroke the bared line of her throat and Joanna was unable to suppress the shiver his touch caused in veins that coursed with sudden excitement. 'And not only to me. I know men well enough to recognise the signs when a woman's turning them on.'

'Stop that!' Her hand clutched the back of his, stilling its provocative movement, and held on to it. 'I—I didn't turn anybody on, as you so crudely put it. If they were, it was entirely of their own making. And I—I didn't run my fingers through anybody's hair except—except yours.'

'Oh? Well, supposing that's true, why was I singled out for favour?'

'I don't know,' she shrugged impatiently, dropping her hand away from his. 'It was—just one of those things a person does on impulse.'

'I see. So I'm wrong in thinking it might have been something to do with Paula?'

'Paula?'

'My—soon-to-be wife.'

Joanna's voice sank into faintness. 'Why should P-Paula interest me?'

'For the same reason she interests my sister Liz,' he returned drily.

Joanna's throat felt cool when he took his hand away and unbuttoned his suit jacket, enlarging the shimmering white area of his shirt. Then his hand came back, the fingers lifting a silken strand of her hair and letting it slide through them before their tips touched sensuously on her cheek, her involuntarily closed eyelids, her smooth-skinned jawline and, finally, her trembling lips as he murmured: 'But maybe I should thank Liz this time. She's never sent anybody before who had hair like spun silk, skin as smooth as rose petals and eyes like violets ... and a mouth I want to kiss every time I see it, even when it's lying to me.'

'But I——'

Joanna parted her lips to protest and Alex took forceful advantage of that fact, closing his own over them in shocking impact so that her senses were numbed for long moments as he moved his mouth abrasively on hers. His hands augmented the sensual force of his lips, seeking and finding the firmed rise of her breasts under the filmy gauze of her dress, and provoking a sudden wild storm of response in her which she was too inexperienced to control.

The tremor in her hands stilled as they crept over his white shirt and held to the silky material like a drowning man clutching for straws. Then, like homing pigeons, they undid three of the shirt buttons and slid inside, pressing themselves to the moist heat of his hard-muscled chest, feeling the increase of her own heartbeat to match the erratic thump of his under her palm.

'Alex ...' she breathed when his mouth lifted and went savagely to leave fiery imprints on the cool whiteness of her shoulder and pulsing neck before plunging to the softly scented valley between her breasts. 'Please ...'

She didn't know what it was she begged him for, but

without her conscious willing, her hands left his shirt and slid up over the wide expanse of his tough-muscled shoulders to stroke through the thick wiriness of his hair before touching his hard-fleshed face and cupping his firm jaw to bring his head back to hers again.

His eyes blazed almost accusingly as they went over her disordered cloud of hair, then touched on her eyes, her cheeks, her mouth with an impact nearly physical. His chest rising and falling with his heavy breathing, he spread one hand along the side of Joanna's face.

'Quite the little witch, aren't you?' he mocked softly. His fingers tightened on her skin. 'You could make a man forget every scruple he has.'

With his words, the mesmeric effect his eyes had been having on Joanna was cleanly cut off. His insinuation was clear enough. If he had not been so high-principled, their lovemaking would have taken a deeper, more final course. Struggling up and away from him, she jerked her face away from his hand and tugged the sleeves of her dress up over her shoulders.

'Paula being the main scruple,' she snapped tartly.

His brows went up, her anger seemingly having no more effect on him than a summer storm. 'You could say that,' he drawled laconically, straightening up himself and buttoning the front of his shirt while Joanna's cheeks burned in embarrassed remembrance of her eager searching inside it. 'But I wasn't particularly thinking of Paula.' His hands went up to smooth his hair with a quick, practised motion.

'Then you should have been! You're engaged to the woman, for heaven's sake, although I noticed you haven't given her a ring to mark the occasion!'

Alex shrugged and slid back under the wheel, preparatory to opening his door. 'Paula and I went that route once before.'

'And rings aren't necessary the second time around?'

'In this case, no.'

'Well, Paula's a lot different from me!' Joanna bit off sharply. 'If you were engaged to me, I'd make sure the whole world knew it and that you wouldn't be so inclined to rush off to the nearest female when we'd had a row!'

'A row?'

She flashed him a caustic look. 'I'm not exactly a simpleton! It only needed half an eye to see that you had the daggers drawn between you tonight. And I don't like being used as a tool for revenge!'

With that, she opened her door and propelled herself from the car. Alex caught up with her at the front door, swinging her round by the arm to face him. He was angry, she could see by the white lines at either side of his mouth.

'You little idiot! Do you think that if I wanted revenge—which I don't!—I'd have used you or any other woman to get it? I demand as much honesty from myself as I do from others—which, by the way,' he gritted as he threw open the door and stood aside to let her pass, 'is why *you* will never be engaged to me! I could never live with a woman who can't distinguish between truth and fiction.'

Joanna swept past him, unexpected tears rushing to her eyes. Blinking with her back to him, she said in a choked voice: '*That's* a problem you'll never have, Mr Harper, because I—I wouldn't marry you if you grovelled at my f-feet and begged me.'

'And that's not likely to happen either!' he snapped,

drawing level with her in his quick strides to the study when Nick's voice halted him.

'I thought I heard the car come in a while ago—where have you two been?' Standing at the far end of the hall, near the kitchen door, his eyes took in Joanna in her flame-coloured dress, her hair attractively ruffled from Alex's lovemaking. His soft whistle and involuntary: 'Wow!' were reminiscent of Glen's puppylike enthusiasm on occasion. 'You look—fantastic, Anna!'

'Thanks,' Joanna acknowledged tightly, and walked towards Nick. 'Your brother took pity on me and insisted I go out to Peter Erikson's birthday dinner party with him and Paula.'

'I've just made some coffee, would you like some?' Nick half turned back to where Alex still stood in the middle of the hall. 'Alex?'

'Not for me, thanks. I've had enough for one night.'

His words had a meaning far and beyond Nick's comprehension, and Joanna sent Alex a scathing look before following Nick to the kitchen. There, she automatically took over the setting out of cups and pouring of the coffee Nick had made. Her fingers were shaking so much that some of the coffee spilled over in a saucer, and she berated herself as she emptied the excess into the sink.

Okay, Alex Harper had made more of an impression on her than any other man had in her short life. He had made her more conscious of herself as a woman, one who could abandon herself to the dictates of her senses in a way she had never known before. Sooner or later, such a man would have had to come along. It just happened that this one could never enter her life on a permanent basis. He had Paula, the one he had no doubt been in love with for years, the one who would share the beautifully modern new house with him.

Taking the cups to the table, where Nick had taken his customary place at her right, she resolutely decided to put Alex from her mind completely as a man. He would be her employer for another few weeks, then she would go away from Clearwater and with luck never see him again.

'Thanks,' Nick gave a half-hearted grin, and it was only then that she realised how quiet he had been, how preoccupied he now seemed.

'Is anything wrong, Nick? I thought you were staying at Shirley's tonight.'

He added sugar and cream to his cup and stirred slowly before replying. 'I was supposed to, but—well, we had kind of an argument and I thought it would be better if I came home.'

'Oh. Well,' Joanna forced a measure of levity into her voice, 'I've heard that premarital jitters can be a scary thing. And it's not long now until you and Shirley get married, is it?'

'After tonight, I wonder if we should get married at all,' he said gloomily, lifting his cup to a mouth that had a heart-tugging resemblance to Alex's.

'Don't be silly,' she chided him briskly. 'I've never known two people more suited than you and Shirley. You're both——' she shrugged, 'nice people.'

The ghost of a smile played at the back of his brown eyes as he looked at her and said: 'You're nice people too. How come you don't have some good-looking fellow dangling on your string?'

An involuntary sadness swept over Joanna, and Nick evidently noticed the change in her expression. Leaning across the table, he said: 'There's somebody, isn't there? And I'd guess the damned fool isn't somebody you left behind in Vancouver, because you didn't look like this when you first came here.' With an abrupt change of subject, he asked thoughtfully: 'What had you and Alex been arguing about before you came in?'

Joanna gave him a nervous sideways glance, then looked down into her half empty cup. 'Alex? What makes you think we'd been arguing?'

Evenly, he returned: 'Because you looked as if you'd been pulled through a hay baler, and Alex looked— madder than I've seen him in a long time.'

She shrugged. 'He wasn't in a good mood because he and Paula had had an argument of some kind. She wasn't too happy either when we left the club.'

Nick gave an unexpected chuckle. 'That doesn't surprise me! I guess she wasn't too happy when he insisted on taking you out with them.' His voice dropped a notch. 'You really do look fabulous tonight, Anna. If I'd driven you home, I'd have been tempted to stop the car and——'

He stopped abruptly, understanding coming into his eyes, and Joanna quickly lifted her cup to drain the coffee.

'He did stop the car and make a pass at you, didn't he?' he said slowly, a frown gathering between his brows. 'That's why you were so long outside when you got back. Damn him,' he exploded with a violence unusual to his pacific nature, 'and he'd just left Paula.'

'It's all right,' Joanna said nervously, getting up to carry their cups to the percolator for a refill. 'It was because he'd quarrelled with Paula that he—he——'

'Made love to you? What kind of an excuse is that? Hell, I'm going to go in there and——'

'No, please, Nick.' Joanna's hand on his forearm halted his rush into the study to confront Alex. 'It was— my fault—as much as his.'

Nick stared down into her anguished eyes for interminable moments before saying, visibly shaken: 'My God, it's him, isn't it? You've fallen for Alex.'

Too overwrought to argue the point, Joanna nodded mutely and a look that was half compassionate, half angry, crossed his features. It seemed a natural thing that he should slide his arms around her and pull her head to the sheltering comfort of his chest.

'Oh, Anna,' he sighed brokenly, 'you couldn't have chosen anybody worse than Alex to fall in love with! Apart from Paula, who's been in his life from the year zero, he thinks Liz sent you here to take him away from her. And he's not going to give in to Liz now any more than he did before with the other girls she sent.'

Joanna lifted her head, her eyes flashing when she said angrily: 'But Liz *didn't* send me here for that reason! I—happened to be there the night Alex called and said she'd have to come and take care of things here. She didn't want to come, because of her business and——' she paused, then went on: 'Well, she didn't want to come, and she knew that I was looking for a job and that I'd taken a cooking course——'

'You had?' he interjected in such amazement that she saw the humour of it and clarified:

'A course in gourmet cookery. That didn't really prepare me for a housekeeping job on a ranch, but I—I really wanted the job.'

'I know,' he said soberly, 'Alex told us about your father being out of work.'

Conscience smote Joanna again, though part of her wondered in anguish why Alex had believed that about her but not that Liz's intentions were strictly practical.

'That wasn't the important thing,' she sighed, 'it was

just that ... well, I wanted to prove to myself that I could do something worthwhile, hold my own in a regular job ...'

Tears thickened her voice and Nick drew her closer to him, brown eyes warm with sympathy as they looked down into hers. Awareness that he was holding her closely, intimately, seemed to come to both of them at the same time.

'Anna?' he whispered, puzzled.

Joanna herself seemed mesmerised as she accepted the touch of his lips on hers. All she was aware of was a deep fondness for the man who kissed her with none of the fierce passion his brother had shown such a short time before. Nick was kind, gentle, compassionate ... and Shirley was a lucky girl. She must have murmured something of that thought when Nick raised his head to look at her again, bemusement clouding his eyes, for Alex's voice came stonily from the door.

'Shirley might not think herself so lucky if she could see what's going on now,' he said harshly and, as if he had doused them with icy water, Nick and Joanna drew hastily apart and looked with startled eyes in his direction.

# CHAPTER EIGHT

ALEX had taken off his tie and rolled up the sleeves of his shirt over muscular forearms, but he still exuded an air of righteous formality. The brown eyes that could seem so warm, so lit with the vitality pulsing in his big frame, were bleak and cold as they went contemptuously from Joanna's flushed cheeks to Nick's stunned expression.

Yet it was Nick who recovered more quickly than Joanna.

'You're a fine one to talk!' he said belligerently, taking a step towards Alex with bunched fists that threatened violence. 'What about——'

Joanna put a warning hand on his arm and his head swung back to her, his eyes blazing.

'Please, Nick,' she begged softly, 'let me take care of it.'

Something in the dark violet of her eyes must have got through to him, because he turned after a moment and went swiftly across the room, brushing past Alex in the doorway without looking at him again.

A quiver of what could have been excitement or alarm went through Joanna when Alex crossed the kitchen to her side. Forcing her eyes up to his face, she saw that the outline of his well-made lips were rigid, his eyes as cold as they had been from the other side of the room.

'So how are you going to take care of it—or me, as you obviously meant?' he jeered, voice granite-hard.

Joanna focused her gaze on the opened neck of his shirt, where the powerful column of his neck started. 'What happened between Nick and me,' she began quietly, 'was my fault entirely. He——'

'That doesn't surprise me one bit, considering your record this evening,' he grated, the words seeming like steel chips in his mouth. 'I'd advise that in future you confine your amorous activities to men not committed elsewhere. This isn't the city, where it seems anything goes.'

Hurt anger flashed through her as her head jerked up. 'And all you Cariboo men are such fragile creatures you can't resist the lure of a newcomer?' she mocked.

'Not when she looks like you.'

She laughed scornfully. 'My goodness, you're really boosting my self-esteem! Maybe I should pack my bags and try Hollywood!'

'I wouldn't,' he rejoined drily, turning away to walk to the door. 'You'd make a lousy actress.'

This hit Joanna where she had been hurting for a long time. It was almost as if he knew of her disastrous foray into Shakespeare.

'And, by the way, you can add Pete Erikson to the list of men otherwise committed,' Alex sent his parting shot from the doorway, and disappeared before Joanna had time to register more than the bald statement.

But even indignation had no power to straighten her slumped shoulders as she poured coffee into her cup and carried it to the table. Sighing, she settled back into her chair, elbows on the table, hands cupping her face.

What an idiot she had been to let herself get into such a vulnerable state over a man ... a man who could wound her to the depths with one glance from his brown eyes. Yet did anyone really have a choice as to where they would bestow their love? Of which lips would be the ones to set fire to the senses of another?

Alex had said he wanted to kiss her mouth, even when it lied to him. But that was a purely physical male reaction. She wasn't so inexperienced with the opposite sex that she didn't know that a man could be aroused physically by a woman without necessarily feeling the emotion of love. The love, so important to a woman, that made her want to cleave to her man's side, helping and encouraging him through the ups and downs of life, bearing his children and caring for them until their maturity.

Another sigh broke from her, and she lifted her cup to trembling lips. Even though she felt all these things for Alex, nothing could ever come of it. The web of half-truths, the network of duplicity she had been forced to maintain at Clearwater, could never be explained away to a man like Alex. He would never be able to trust her, as he had told her earlier.

Through a blur of tears, Joanna wished fervently that she had never met Liz Harper on that spring day in Vancouver.

On Monday Alex took her into town, but there was no mention of lunch as he had planned for Saturday. His manner was coolly polite, as it had been all weekend, when he suggested the trip at breakfast. About to refuse, Joanna found herself numbed into nodding acquiescence when he said:

'I presume you'll want to send something of your pay-check to your family to help out while your father's out of work.'

In the post office she was compelled, under his watchful eye, to take out a money order for half the amount and seal it in an envelope which she hesitantly addressed to her father at the penthouse address. To her relief, Alex decided to collect the Clearwater mail while she hurriedly pushed the envelope into the mailbox.

'You have a parcel,' he said cryptically as he joined her at the main door of the post office, handing her a box-shaped package and a large manila envelope, both addressed in unfamiliar handwriting and with no return address that she could see.

'Why don't you have a coffee while I see to my business?' he suggested practically, with no hint of any feelings either way on the subject.

Joanna was in no mood to do any kind of shopping, so she nodded without speaking and entered the coffee shop they had halted at before, taking a booth towards the back. While the waitress poured her coffee, she ripped open the manila envelope and brought out several letters that had been addressed to the penthouse, and a scrawled note from Liz.

'J. As arranged, I've collected your mail and here it is. Hope all goes well at Clearwater—guess it must be going smoothly, because I haven't had an irate call or letter from big brother, and I'm sure he would have let me know if you were in any way deficient! So maybe I was thinking along the right lines when I sent you out there.

'The tablecloth (which I'll not enquire into too deeply) is on its way separately. Think it's the same as the one you want to replace. Am crazily busy right now, so can't write more. Happy hunting! Liz.'

Joanna sipped slowly at her coffee and thought deeply about Liz's letter, particularly the two sentences that had seemed to leap from the page. 'Maybe I was thinking along the right lines when I sent you out there,' and 'Happy hunting.' Read through a biased eye, either or both could mean that Liz had deliberately planned what Alex suspected—that his sister had sent Joanna to Clearwater with one purpose in mind. To snare him.

Abstractedly she opened the other letters, all three of them bearing foreign postmarks. With only half her attention she scanned the enthusiastic reports of her father and Marie as they described Italy, France, Britain.

Glancing up as she reached the end of the last letter, she saw Alex's broad shoulders silhouetted against the café door and quickly stuffed the letters back into the large envelope. By the time he had looked around and located her, coming with his long stride towards her booth, Joanna was sipping innocently at her coffee.

'Your business didn't take long,' she remarked coolly as he settled his big frame opposite her.

'The man I wanted to see wasn't there,' he returned nonchalantly. 'It's not that important, I can see him another time.'

The waitress, all too visibly impressed with his air of masculinity, rushed to take his order. And as if all too used to feminine susceptibility, he gave her a lazy smile and ordered what amounted to a second breakfast—pancakes with maple syrup and coffee.

'You have the biggest appetite of any man I know,' Joanna remarked tartly when the waitress had brought his coffee and replenished her own cup.

One brow quirked up as he stirred his cup. 'In more ways than one,' he agreed laconically, a meaning smile lifting the corners of his firm mouth.

Colour swept unbidden to Joanna's cheeks, and she busied herself with the adding of sugar and cream to her coffee. It was obvious which of the appetites he referred to, and she could well believe that one woman would be hard put to satisfy that particular appetite in him. Somehow, she couldn't imagine that Paula was that woman, but she said tongue-in-cheek:

'I'm sure Paula will be able to satisfy all your needs, whatever they are.'

'You could be right.' His gaze fell on the package she had propped against the wall. 'You're most unusual for a woman. You haven't even peeked into the parcel to see what's in it.'

'I know what's in it,' she snapped.

'Oh? And how about those airmail love letters sticking out of that envelope?'

Joanna put her cup down quickly, her eyes swivelling to the manila envelope and the corner of red and blue airmail pattern on one of her father's letters which she had obviously failed to tuck far enough in.

'My personal mail is none of your business,' she said stiffly, lifting the large envelope and placing it on the seat beside her.

'Agreed.' He smiled again at the waitress who reappeared at that moment to place a stack of pancakes before him. 'We'll have some more coffee, too, while you're here.'

Resuming their conversation as if it had never been interrupted, he said in a voice pleasantly conversational: 'But I must admit you intrigue me, Anna. You surround yourself with mystery, and you obviously wouldn't have gone without male interest before you came here. So what happened? Did you have a fight and he went off to join the Foreign Legion?' Smiling, he tackled the daunting pile of pancakes after pouring maple syrup generously over them.

'He's—travelling ... on business,' she conceded, wondering why it was so easy to pile up semi-truths to small mountain size.

There was no more conversation between them as Alex, his face sober, methodically demolished the pancakes. The waitress gave him a tremulous return smile when he paid the bill, and cast a half puzzled glance at Joanna, as if she had noticed the strained silence between them at the table.

After calling in at the supermarket, where they picked up much-needed supplies, Alex headed the car back to the ranch. When they had left the paved streets behind he said casually:

'So what happens when your business traveller gets back? You aiming to marry him?'

Joanna, intent on checking her shopping list, looked up at him in surprise. There was a bland expression in the brown eyes shaded by his stockman's hat. Did he really care if she married another man, or was this just an extension of his curiosity about her? Sighing, she decided on the latter.

'That would be difficult.'

'He's married already?'

'Yes.'

She saw his quick glance at her downcast face, but refused to meet what might be compassion in the warm brown of his eyes. Swallowing hard, she wondered miserably how much deeper the pit of deceit would have to go before she left Clearwater. Now she had let Alex believe that she had been having an affair with a married man. If it weren't so tragic, it could be uproariously funny.

The rest of that week passed in a whirl of frenzied

activity for Joanna. Warding off the sense of guilt that
assailed her, she scrubbed and baked and polished until
the old house gleamed complacently and the Harper
men loosened their belts at the end of a meal in happy
discomfort. Often, she would look up to find Alex's eyes
on her in concentrated bemusement, and that would be
her cue to jump up and initiate a further totally unneces-
sary activity.

Dusty and her offspring had been moved to more permanent quarters in the barn at the beginning of the
week, so she had scoured her room from top to bottom
until it smelled no more of dog but disinfectant. As their
crying had disturbed her sleep earlier, now the absence
of it made her nights restless.

The tablecloth Liz had sent to replace the one Joanna
had long ago consigned to the incinerator near the house
wasn't quite of the same design in its lace edge, but she
doubted if any of the Harper men would notice that.
No comment had been made, even by Alex, on the
evening she had spread its snowy whiteness on the table.

On Friday she was standing back to admire the deep
shine she had created on the hall floor when Shirley's
voice sent her twirling around to issue a warning about
stepping on the newly polished tiles.

'All right,' the blonde girl returned, laughing. 'Then
you come out here.'

Which Joanna did, picking her way carefully over the
areas she knew to be dry. When she reached the kitchen,
she found that Shirley had already plugged in the percolator for fresh coffee.

'Oh, I could do with that,' she sighed, flopping into
one of the chairs by the table.

'If you ask me,' Shirley eyed her severely, taking the
seat opposite, 'you're taking this housekeeping bit far

too seriously. Who cares about a footprint showing in the hall?'

'Alex does,' Joanna replied briefly, hitching her aching feet on to an adjoining chair. A camaraderie had grown up between the two girls during the several visits Shirley had made to Clearwater since Joanna's arrival.

'Does it matter so much what he thinks?' Shirley enquired with loftily lifted brows. 'After all, you're doing a lot more on your own than the regular housekeeper ever used to do. At least she had help with the laundry and heavy chores around the place.'

'She did?'

'Sure. Most of the ranch wives have helped in the main house at one time or another.' Almost casually, Shirley threw in: 'I was talking to a couple of them on my way here. They said Alex had told them to leave you strictly alone, that you didn't like interference in the house.'

'He said *what*?'

Shirley was apologetic. 'I guess they took him at his word. None of them has been near you since you came?'

Joanna shook her head. She had wondered about the aloofness of the ranch women in their neatly contoured bungalows at the far side of the working area. Now it was becoming abundantly clear that Alex had been the fox among the chickens.

'Why would he do that?' she asked absently, answering her own question silently almost as soon as it was voiced. He had thought to break her by laying on her a burden of housekeeping he knew she wasn't equipped or qualified to deal with. But she had bested him, she told herself with weary triumph. The house sparkled from attic to cellar as he had specified, and there had been few complaints about her cooking lately.

'I don't pretend to understand him,' Shirley intruded into her thoughts. 'He keeps everything into himself, all the things that matter.' She was silent for a moment, then burst out: 'I wish he wouldn't marry Paula! Can you imagine me sitting talking to her like this?'

'Only if you bowed at regular intervals to acknowledge her superiority,' Joanna chuckled, getting up as the percolator signalled its readiness. 'But it's pretty important that you keep on the right side of her, if she's going to be Alex's wife.'

'I hate her,' Shirley said in a low voice. 'I can't imagine what Alex sees in her. Oh, she's beautiful and all the rest, but beauty's a lot more than skin deep. I wish Alex would fall for somebody like you.'

Joanna gave a tinkling laugh. 'No chance, honey. Paula's had her hooks into him for a long, long time, and besides——' she halted, then forced a smile as she carried their cups to the table, 'I have my own plans for the future.'

Shirley looked up at her pensively, her eyes following the petite figure on its way to sit opposite her. 'I thought from what Nick said, Alex might figure in your future if it wasn't for Paula.' She looked down at her hands clasped on the table top. 'I—I know about—I know that Nick kissed you, Anna.'

'It didn't mean anything,' Joanna denied swiftly, her eyes urgent on Shirley's.

'I know that too,' the other girl smiled. 'Nick explained that he was upset about our argument, and that you——'

'That I needed a strong male shoulder to lean on for a minute or two,' Joanna finished softly for her. 'Nick really is a wonderful guy, and I'd really go for him if I didn't know how much he loves you.'

'And I'd scratch your eyes out if I ever thought you

were casting lecherous thoughts in his direction!' There was a belying sparkle in Shirley's eyes, then she went on soberly: 'I really do wish you and Alex would get together. Apart from anything else, it would be great for Glen. After what happened last year——'

'What did happen last year? All I've heard is an innuendo here and there.'

Shirley looked embarrassed. 'Well, I—I shouldn't really have brought that up. It's just that——' she raised her head to look squarely into Joanna's eyes, 'well, last year there was a girl. She got in touch with Alex and told him that Glen was the—the father of the baby she was expecting. Naturally, Alex was upset. But when he looked into it, he found that Glen had been telling the truth. He'd been—seeing this girl, but so had a great many others, closer to the crucial time. Glen just happened to come from the most prosperous family her father could fix on. If it hadn't been for Alex ...' Her shudder was eloquent.

Joanna was stunned. No wonder Alex was keeping a strict eye on his younger brother! And she, like an idiot, had told him that Glen should be allowed to grow up and make his own decisions. Had even asked him if his father had kept such close tabs on him. Now that she knew the circumstances, the question seemed ridiculous. Despite his experience with women, Alex would never leave himself open to such an accusation.

She only half heard the remainder of Shirley's conversation, and she was still thoughtful when the other girl took her leave on Bunty.

If Alex hadn't been so coldly disapproving when he came to tell Joanna that Peter Erikson wanted to speak to her, she would probably never have agreed to the dinner and dance date with him on Saturday evening. But with Alex pacing round the study while she spoke with Peter, puffing furiously on one of his aromatic cigars, she forced herself into a delighted acceptance.

'I'd love to, Peter. About seven?'

Alex forestalled her as she was leaving the room, coming to lean with his back to the door, effectively blocking her exit.

'Another admirer?'

'Another *friend*,' she emphasised, adding: 'Not that it's any of your business.'

'Your sex life is your own business,' he agreed frigidly, ignoring her outraged gasp, 'but it becomes mine when it's conducted under my roof.'

Spluttering, Joanna gazed at him speechlessly for the space of several erratic heartbeats before bursting out: 'When do I have the chance to conduct any kind of life under your roof apart from scrubbing, polishing, cooking and cleaning? Look at my hands!' She thrust their work-reddened surfaces before him and had the satisfaction of seeing him wince.

'I'm aware that your work nowadays can't be faulted,' he conceded grimly, averting his eyes from her hands as if they pained him. 'When I said "under my roof" I meant, of course, while you're living in my house. I'm responsible for your behaviour, which——' he stressed heavily, 'I have good reason to know personally can be quite—uninhibited at times.'

'How *dare* you!' Joanna's eyes grew into wide blue orbs of disbelief. 'It was you who ... who ...'

'Don't let's go into the outraged maiden bit again,' he interrupted caustically, his mouth a thinned line. 'And don't try to tell me that your married lover hasn't made love to you a lot more—intimately than I have.'

Joanna stared at him blankly. 'My what?'

'Forgotten him already? Don't you care about the man's ego?'

Her mouth closed with a snap. 'Not one bit in that respect! Now will you please let me pass? I still have work to do in the kitchen.'

Without another word, he stepped aside and even opened the door for her, albeit with a derisive air.

He was a devil, she decided, fuming as she returned to her own domain at the rear of the house. A devil who regarded every female as fair game—except the one he was in love with. Not once in her presence had he put a hand wrong with Paula. And why should he? He had waited years for her, a few weeks or months made no difference either way. Meanwhile, he could pass his amorous time with girls like herself, foolish enough to fall in love with him.

Peter called for her on Saturday evening in a car that seemed conservative for his ebullient nature ... really, she would have expected that Alex's taste ran more to the family sized vehicle, and that Peter would have owned the powerful sports car possessed by Alex.

Probably it was his one concession to flamboyance, she thought snappishly as she went down the steps to smile at Peter. She was conscious of Alex's eyes on her in a gaze that smouldered against the flimsy flame of the only dressy dress she had brought with her.

The smile she directed at Peter was especially radiant for Alex's benefit. And Peter looked scrubbed and attractive in white shirt and red tie under a blazer of dark navy, as if he had been specially careful in his grooming for this date.

Joanna herself had taken great care with her own appearance, arranging her hair in a smooth chignon at her nape in a way that added several years to her age, she hoped. Make-up she had confined mainly to her eyes, enlarging and dramatising them ... that she had been successful was evident in Alex's initial stunned appraisal when she crossed the hall as he came from his study. Thrilling to her success, she had only abstractedly noted that he, too, was dressed for an evening out in well-tailored tan safari suit and acid lemon silk polo shirt.

Joanna moved on again across the hall when the sound of Peter's arrival came through the front door standing open to the breeze.

'You look good enough to eat,' he enthused, grinning as he grasped her hands and held them out from her sides.

'If I'd known you'd feel that way,' Joanna said, wide-eyed, 'I'd never have accepted your invitation to dinner!'

'Don't worry,' he laughed, 'I wouldn't be so foolish. That would really be cutting off my nose to spite my face.'

Still holding Joanna's hands as if reluctant to let them go, he turned his head to nod at Alex, still standing on the porch steps and watching them with enigmatic eyes.

'You and Paula going out tonight?'

'Yes.'

'Anywhere special?'

'Probably to the same place as you,' Alex returned drily. 'We don't have that many special places to eat and dance around here.' He stepped down to join them. 'We'll probably see you there.'

This thought seemed not to please Peter, but he forced a hearty: 'Sure' as he dropped Joanna's hands and glanced at his watch. 'We'd better be on our way. I made a reservation, but it gets pretty crowded on Saturday and they may not hold it.' Opening the passenger door for Joanna, he handed her into the car and with a casual

'See you' to Alex, went round and slid into the driver's seat.

At the last minute, Alex leaned down to speak to him across Joanna through the open window. 'How's Verna? Isn't she due back soon?'

Joanna glanced quickly at Peter, her eyes widening when she saw fingers of dull red creeping up under his skin.

'As far as I know she's fine,' he said stiffly at last. 'I believe she's due back next week.'

'Good. You must be looking forward to having her home after so long.' With a slap of his hand against the roof as a signal of farewell, he straightened away from the car. The transmision gears jammed as Peter slammed against the lever, but in another moment they were speeding down the half-mile driveway to the road.

Knowing that she had to say something to relieve the atmosphere, or the evening would be a complete ruin, Joanna said tentatively:

'Is—Verna somebody special?'

Peter spared her a quick sideways look, the flinty cast in his eyes disappearing when they met the darker blue of hers.

On the way in to the roadhouse, Peter told her about the girl he had been dating before her trip to Europe. 'There's nothing definite between us, as Alex implied.' His mouth tightened again as he turned back to the road. 'I can't understand why he felt he had to mention Verna right then, unless ...'

'Unless what?'

'Unless he's interested in *you*,' Peter continued thoughtfully, lifting his brows when Joanna laughed.

'I can eliminate that as his reason,' she scorned. 'I'm the last one he would waste his interest on. According to

him, I'm totally unreliable, untrustworthy and hopelessly
incompetent.' Although, she added silently, he had told
her a couple of times lately that her skills had improved
in the household department.

'Untrustworthy?' Peter frowned. 'How come? Have
you been helping yourself to the family silver or something?'

'Hardly! No, it's just that—oh, well, it doesn't matter.
But I can assure you that Alex doesn't have a jealous
bone in his body where I'm concerned. Besides, he's
going to marry your sister, isn't he?'

'I don't know,' he said slowly, negotiating the mended
bridge over the creek. 'Sometimes I think he'll never for-
give Paula for letting him down before, when his parents
died. And I have to admit that a good wife was what
he needed right then. Alex isn't the kind who forgives
and forgets very easily.'

'Well, I think you're wrong,' Joanna stated, then fell
silent as she watched the trees slide by on either side.
If the new house was to be a surprise for Paula, then
presumably her brother would know nothing about it
either.

After that, she tried to put Alex out of her mind, at
least for that evening. She was succeeding very well
in that object, too, when she looked up one time, laughing at one of the stories Peter was telling her, and felt
a stab of shock as her eyes met the narrowed brown of
his. For a moment or two it seemed as if Alex and she
were alone in a vacuum, then she rallied by sneering inwardly that of course the mighty Alex Harper would
command one of the best tables in the house, one bordering the dance floor.

Strangely, Joanna felt more relaxed in conversation
with Peter than in dancing with him. His wit came to

the fore after a couple of tension-easing drinks, and several times Joanna's laugh rang out, her smiling mouth sobering each time she met Alex's disapproving stare. But the unaccustomed amount of alcohol had its effect on her also, and her own stares back at Alex became bolder, more challenging as time wore on.

He seemed disinclined for dancing himself this evening, taking Paula on to the floor only occasionally, and he appeared not to mind when she was asked to dance by what looked like old friends.

He was smoking a lot, she noted when he lit his third cigar, dismissing the thought from her mind when Peter launched into another tale from his past ... tales which, unfortunately, always involved Alex as well as himself.

An Alex very different from the one who had emerged after his parents' death. A fun-loving, girl-chasing, uninhibited Alex ... one she found it hard to credit. From the words Peter didn't say, she gathered that Alex had been much more successful with girls than he had, but he seemed not to resent that fact, and his earlier anger towards Alex seemed forgotten.

Then, in the middle of a particularly funny story, Peter's eyes strayed to a point over Joanna's shoulder and his words ceased abruptly, his jaw dropping in disbelief.

'My God!' he breathed unevenly. 'Verna!'

'Verna?'

'She's here. She must have come back sooner than expected.'

Joanna glanced over her shoulder and saw a slim brunette in a turquoise sheath dress seating herself beside a slightly older couple at a table not far away. She turned back quickly to look at Peter, his expression open for all to see. He was in love with the dark girl, that much was evident from the surprised longing in his eyes.

Desperately she cast around in her mind for plausible reasons for Peter to be sitting here with another girl, but her brain seemed suddenly sluggish. There was little relief in the recognition that Alex had appeared suddenly at their side.

'Go over and see Verna,' he urged Peter. 'Tell her you're here with Paula and me—and my housekeeper, Anna, of course.'

Peter looked dazedly up at his friend before comprehension dawned. 'Hell, Alex, I'm not dumping Anna because Verna chooses to come back early without letting me know!'

'Don't be a fool! She probably thought it would be a nice surprise for you ... instead of which, she's going to be unpleasantly surprised herself to see you out with——' his eyes flickered contemptuously over Joanna, 'somebody else.'

'No!' Peter ground out angrily. 'What do you think I am, that I'd insult Anna that way?'

They were speaking as if she didn't exist, and although she rebelled inwardly at the thought of sharing the table with Alex and Paula, she laid an entreating hand on Peter's sleeve.

'You wouldn't be insulting me, Peter, honestly,' she said earnestly. 'I understand, really I do.' Attempting a lighter note, she added: 'What kind of a girl do you think I am, that I'd come between a man and his woman?'

Ignoring the sharp downward turn of Alex's head, she concentrated instead on putting as much sincerity as she could muster into her blue-eyed gaze across the table to Peter. To her relief, he at last untensed and covered her hand in a grateful squeeze.

'You're a peach, Anna.' Glancing at Alex as he rose, he enquired: 'You'll take care of her?'

'She's my responsibility,' Alex returned, equally taut.

Then Peter was gone, and Joanna felt her hand being taken and her body helped from the seat.

'We'd better dance this one, then you can come back to my table.' Alex put a hand on her waist to urge her forward to where the small dance floor was already crowded, and she had no option but to follow him.

She was stiff in his arms when they took to the floor, a thunderous look from Paula as she danced past with her partner doing nothing to relax the taut state of her muscles. But gradually, as they moved with enforced slowness in the small space, the warmth from Alex's body permeated hers with a kind of inertia, so that her slight form relaxed against him and his arm grew almost protective round her.

There were no words for a long time, and Joanna was dreamily content to let herself drift on a tide of unrealisable fantasies. Paula didn't exist, and Alex had brought her here to celebrate her ecstatic acceptance of his marriage proposal. A future of unbounded rosiness lay before them ... the rafters at Clearwater would ring with their children's laughter ... lots of children. Didn't ranchers need many children to make the ranch a family affair?

Alex had to voice his question twice before she jerked her head away from the lean curve of his cheek.

'What?'

'I asked if you meant what you said about not coming between a man and his woman?' he reiterated, eyes sober in the dimmed light.

The cold reality of what he was asking doused Joanna's daydreams like a bucket of water thrown on a campfire. This was the crux of the disagreement between them since her arrival in ranch country, his belief that Liz had sent her here as a wedge between himself and Paula.

Weary suddenly of the long-drawn-out battle, Joanna said in a flat voice: 'I meant every word of it. Where's the point in falling for a man who's already committed elsewhere?'

'Where indeed?' he returned with equal flatness, but his arm drew her closer again and they danced the remainder of the number in as close proximity as any of the other couples.

Alex's quietly spoken explanations back at the table, where he had installed Joanna, did little to soften the knife edge of hostility in Paula's eyes, and when they all left a short while later, she enveloped herself in a sheath of iciness that remained all the way back to her home.

Telling Joanna tersely to get into the front of the car, Alex sprang out and caught up with the incensed Paula near her front door, and spent a long ten minutes talking persuasively to her. From the front seat, Joanna saw the other girl's tanned arms slide up around his neck in an attitude that was almost pleading, and she averted her eyes.

Oh, yes, there was no doubt but that Alex had been concerned—not with her own coming between Peter and his love, but between himself and Paula. Staring straight ahead, she wished that she could merge herself with the shrubbery bordering the Erikson lawns, disappear so that the loving couple could be completely alone.

No sooner had she thought this, however, than Alex was throwing himself into the seat beside her, starting the car and shooting forward along the driveway. Not a word was spoken as they drove the short distance to Clearwater. Alex seemed occupied with his own thoughts, his profile grimly clear cut as he guided the car on the far from even road surface, and Joanna had more than enough to occupy her own thoughts. So much that, when he drew to a halt before the veranda of the house, she gave a start of surprise.

Inside the house, she snapped on the hall lights and started across the hall. The peremptory tone of Alex's voice behind her halted her steps.

'Come into the study, Anna. I want to talk to you.'

# CHAPTER NINE

WOODENLY, Joanna followed Alex into the room she had cleaned thoroughly the previous day. Not a spot marred the deep red surface of the wall-to-wall carpet, and beyond the closed bedroom door she knew that the bed was made up to fresh neatness, the furniture polished to a high gloss, shirts and socks and underwear arranged neatly in drawers and closets.

So he couldn't want to talk about her incompetence in household arts. It must be something to do with Paula. Had she insisted on his getting rid of Joanna as a condition of their making up? Suddenly Joanna didn't care any more. Much better that she should face him with a *fait accompli* rather than the bald assertion of his wish that she should leave Clearwater.

Consequently her voice was cool as she turned by the desk to face him as he came towards her with two glasses in his hands. One he handed to her and she accepted it, knowing that she would need its fiery warmth before many minutes had gone by.

'Anna, I——'

'Alex——'

As they had spoken together, so they stopped together. Alex made a deferentially mocking bow. 'Go ahead. You obviously have something on your mind too.'

'I—yes, I do.' Joanna twisted the long-stemmed glass, which her nose told her held brandy, between her slender fingers. 'I—I think it's best if I leave Clearwater,' she said in a rush.

'Oh?'

The tone was coolly noncommittal, and she gained courage from that. 'Yes, I—I think it would be best all round. I don't seem to be making much headway here.'

As soon as the words left her mouth, she knew they were ridiculously wrong.

'That depends on what kind of headway you'd expected to make in a limited time,' Alex commented drily, turning from her to go and sit heavily in the chair behind the desk. 'I'd say you've done remarkably well in the short time at your disposal.'

She looked at him uncertainly, sensing derision in his tone, yet seeing only blankness in his expression as he stared down into his glass.

'Nothing I do seems right in your eyes,' she said, unable to stop the plaintive note in her voice although she hated it.

'Oh, come on, Anna,' he returned impatiently, rising to pace about the room. 'You're beginning to sound like a mewling pussycat, instead of a girl with a hell of a lot of guts to come out to a ranch and take on the job of housekeeper without having the faintest notion of what such a job entails!'

His restless pacing stopped in front of her, the firm line of his mouth only inches away when he went on: 'It's obvious you didn't have to come all this way from city life to stir up amorous thoughts in male breasts, so what's your game, Anna?' Brown fingers jerked her chin round so that brown eyes could rake her face. 'Who in hell are you, Anna Thomas?—if that's your name!'

'What in hell does it matter to you what my name is, as long as your meals are cooked, your house is kept clean, your laundry done to your satisfaction?' she blazed, then, in a gesture of non-caring, tipped the brandy glass so that its contents surged down her throat until the delicate membranes felt on fire. Banging the glass on the desk, she turned back to face him aggressively.

'You don't care, do you, Alex? As long as Clearwater runs like an oiled clock, you don't give a damn about the people concerned! You care more about that devilish horse of yours than about the woman you're going to marry—and don't tell me you're in love with Paula, because I know you're not!' Unknowingly, her mouth trembled, her eyes glistened with tears. 'A man in love with somebody lights up inside when she comes near—like Peter did tonight when Verna came into the club. But you don't.'

Her inflamed senses noted the sudden clenching of his lean jaw, and she drew a trembling sigh. Now she had left him no choice but to fire her.

Instead she felt his fingers under the chin she had lowered, his husky voice saying, 'But I do.'

'You—you do—what?' she asked, bewildered eyes blinking up into the sudden warmth of his.

His fingers were doing unsettling things with the neat coil of her hair, smoothing then tugging until the anchoring pins fell out and the black tresses swirled round her shoulders.

'I do light up every time she's near me,' he told her gravely, running his fingers freely through the unbound silk of her hair. 'Every time she's near me I want to kiss her lovely mouth, caress her beautiful body, keep her in bed with me for so long that people would say: "Whatever happened to that couple out at Clearwater?"'

'P-Paula *is* beautiful,' she whispered, senses drowning in untold longing when his fingers explored the planes of her face like a blind man seeking for enlightenment.

His voice dropped. 'Who's talking about Paula?' He brought his head down so close that his breath fanned warmly against her mouth.

Joanna stared helplessly into the torrid brown of his eyes, noting for the first time the yellow motes contrasting with the brown, the healthy white surrounding it ... and she was lost.

There was nothing of coquetry in the mouth she raised to his. She loved him, and the action was as natural as a flower tilting towards the sun that gave it life.

And Alex was her life. She realised that in the split second before his mouth gently touched hers. When had she first noted the way his brows, thick but well-shaped, almost met above his eyes? The short hairs, and the russet lashes, were as familiar to her as her own.

Then it didn't matter any more, because Alex was kissing her in a way he never had before. The fingers of his left hand swept through her hair to support her head as his mouth became possessive, parting the trembling softness of her lips and sending explosions of sensual excitement through her veins ... an excitement which conversely brought a weird sensation of lethargy to her limbs, so that her arms slid round his waist and clung there.

Mistily, she felt the zipper of her dress released part way, the folds of flimsy fabric being pushed down over her arms, Alex's muffled curse as he bent to kiss the exposed swell of her flesh. In one effortless movement, he lifted her in his arms and in another moment she felt the coolness of leather as he laid her on the couch.

'I'll have to find you a box to stand on when I kiss you,' he murmured huskily, his eyes alive with a fierce passion as they roved impatiently over her face. 'It won't always be convenient to lie with you like this.'

And lying with her he was. The broad couch easily contained their closely entwined forms, and there was nothing of shyness in Joanna's gesture of sliding her hands round his neck and pulling his head down to the eager parting of her lips. With a half-smothered groan, he took them and moved his own over them in fierce possession ... a possession Joanna longed for in its fullest sense as her body arched to the dominating command in his.

'Alex ... oh, Alex,' she breathed as his mouth left hers and went hotly over the vulnerable exposure of throat and shoulder to breast throbbing from the warm caress of his hand. Freely she responded to the male demand for capitulation, to a need that matched the pulsing command of her own senses.

'So Liz has had her way after all,' Alex murmured, lifting his head as if with an effort to smile whimsically into Joanna's face.

'L-Liz?'

'Sure,' he said with lazy easiness, his fingers smoothing away the black strands of hair from her face. 'It turns out she's getting her own way after all. But you know,' his eyes roamed with unbelievable tenderness over her face, 'I don't give a damn now. I'm just glad that she had the good sense to send you to Clearwater.'

Joanna struggled back to reality, blinking away the dazed dreaminess in her eyes and fixing them on Alex's smiling face ... a face so lit by a luminous glow that she scarcely recognised him. The glow had been ignited by herself, one she would have gloried in under other circumstances. But Alex, like Brutus, was an honourable man. He would not look kindly on a woman he regarded as his being less than truthful in her relationship with him.

'Alex, I——' she began uncomfortably, shifting under the hard outline of his body, 'there's something I should tell——'

The confession she was about to make was interrupted by the harsh burr of the telephone, and she felt him move reluctantly from the closely contoured alignment of their bodies.

'Don't go away,' he said softly, dropping a kiss on her hair before rising and going with his lithe stride to the desk.

'Paula? Something wrong?'

Joanna sat up and glanced over the couch back as she pulled her dress into position and pulled at the zip. Alex's face was a cool mask as he listened to the other woman's voice over the line, but she was so caught up in her own tumultuous feelings that she heard little of his replies.

The most wonderful thing in the world had happened to her tonight in finding that the man she loved returned that feeling in full measure. So why this awful presentiment of catastrophe?

Suddenly, in crushing force, it came to her. Alex loved the girl he believed her to be, a girl of humble background who had overcome her qualms at taking a responsible job without experience in order to help support her unemployed father. Yes, Alex would admire that in a girl ... what he wouldn't find so admirable was the way she had woven a web of untruthfulness about herself.

Shivering, she knew that she would rather have Alex believe that she cared nothing for him than to see his love turn to cold contempt in the knowledge that she had lied consistently since her arrival at Clearwater.

'All right,' Alex sighed into the telephone, 'I'll come

over as usual tomorrow, we'll talk then.'

Joanna had reached the door, her dress securely re-zipped, when Alex reached for her.

'What's the hurry? Don't we have some unfinished business to attend to?'

The touch of his hand on her wrist was like an electric brand, and she pulled away from it. 'Alex, I—I think you may have got the wrong idea ... that is, I—well, I don't want our relationship to go on ... any further ...'

Her voice trailed miserably away at the sudden hardening of his eyes, the tensing of his chin.

'What's that supposed to mean? You were as anxious as me to——'

'Yes, I know,' she interjected hurriedly, feeling for the doorknob behind her back. 'It's just that I——'

'Don't bother to explain,' he said harshly, 'I think I'm bright enough to get the picture. It's the man in Europe, isn't it? You think he'll get a divorce and make an honest woman of you?' The facetious words sounded deadly on his tongue.

'Man——?' Joanna queried uncomprehendingly before she remembered the mythical lover she had let him believe existed to cover up her father's letters to her. 'Yes, that's it. I'd like things to be honest.'

'You could have fooled me!' Sarcasm laced his tone as he took a step back and looked at her with all the contempt she had dreaded. 'Don't worry, Anna, I won't be doing any begging, I've never found it necessary. Your time here will be up soon, so you'll be back in Vancouver about the time he's due back—isn't that the idea?'

'Yes,' she whispered, turning the handle in nerveless fingers and opening the door.

Escaping through the hall to the kitchen, she leaned

heavily on the counter top beside the sinks. All she saw when she raised her head to the window was the pale reflection of her own image, eyes huge round holes in white skin.

Wasn't it better that Alex should think her sojourn at Clearwater had been prompted solely by her wish to pass time until her married love returned? Her mind said yes, but her heart echoed a resounding no.

It was only when she had slid between her bedcovers that she realised the import of what had happened that night. Like the naïve idiot she was, she had imagined that because Alex had made love to her he must be in love with her, that he would want to marry her. But he had said nothing to suggest that ultimate conclusion to their physical passion. On the contrary, he had made a date to see Paula the next day as if nothing untoward was happening in relation to herself.

Of course! To his type of man, rugged and forceful, the conquest of a mere housekeeper would hardly constitute even a small feather in his cap. In his eyes, she had laid herself open to his amorous advances simply by coming here with, as he had believed, his sister's connivance. From her first day at Clearwater, Alex had made it obvious that she attracted him in a physical way, drawing her like a lamb to the slaughter into the orbit of his own sensual attraction.

What would have happened that night if Paula hadn't called? An easy transfer from couch to bed, and a night of sexual bliss? No commitment, just the mutual satisfying of the natural senses.

Thank God for Paula and her timely phone call! Remembering her own submission to the clamour of her alerted senses, she might by now be irrevocably committed to a man whose interest in her was a fleeting thing.

And she knew, with an insight painfully clear, that once Alex Harper had possessed her as a woman, no other man would ever completely satisfy her.

The Ames house was, like its inhabitants as she presently discovered, a rambling riot of differing styles, depending on the tastes of whichever generation had made the additions to the original structure. Nick had told her that the first building had been a store and hostelry, where travellers to and from the Cariboo goldfields were offered succour for the night. Since then, wings had been added haphazardly, giving the house a bizarre but interesting look.

Shirley's open friendliness was reflected in her parents and immediate family, as well as in the innumerable relatives and friends who strayed in and out with bewildering frequency, helping themselves liberally to the constantly restocked buffet table. They chatted avidly among themselves as if they hadn't met for years, and Joanna discovered to her amazement that most of them were regular Sunday visitors, and that she herself was drawn warmly into their conversations. A fleeting pang of regret went through her at the thought of her own sterile childhood by comparison with the young ones who dived noisily between their elders.

It was with reluctance that she at last followed Nick to where their horses were saddled and waiting for them.

'Do we have to leave so soon?' she asked plaintively as Nick helped her on to Sadie's back—the gentle Clearwater mare he had selected for her that morning for the ride over to Shirley's home. 'It seems we've hardly got here.'

He grinned understandingly from Caliph's back. 'Seems that way, I know, but if we don't leave now it's going to be dark before we get home. And Alex would be mad as hell if I kept you out after dark on your first ride.'

Joanna bit back the words that would have disillusioned him on that score, and followed him docilely from the Ames stockyard.

'I think we could go a little faster, don't you?' she asked as they broached a hill and looked back at the Ames spread. 'I feel really safe on Sadie ... she doesn't seem the kind to lose her head.'

'She's not,' Nick agreed easily, though Joanna sensed a longing in him to forsake the deadly dull pace they had pursued until now. 'Sure?' he frowned doubtfully.

At her nod he explained painstakingly what to do, but when Joanna put her heel to the mare she simply increased her speed to an ambling trot.

'Caliph needs more exercise than this,' Joanna said eventually, eyeing the curbed stallion. 'Why don't you run him a little, and I'll catch up with you—finally,' she added wryly.

'He's used to pacing it out with Alex,' Nick apologised with a gentle smile. 'If you're sure you'll be okay, I'll give him his head for a while.' He pointed to the band of trees hazily visible ahead. 'I'll stop there if he'll let me, and wait for you to catch up.'

'In case he doesn't,' she laughed, 'you'd better tell me which way is home.'

Nick described a third of an arc with his arm. 'We're like a wedge,' he said. 'Ames' place behind, Eriksons' dead right, Clearwater more or less ahead.'

Joanna's concern was more real than fancied. The

powerful stallion would be hard to hold once given his head, and although Nick was an expert horseman, Caliph was a one-man animal. An animal with a devil's gleam in his eye, a reflection of the man who owned him.

Caliph's pleasure in being given his head was more than evident in the flow of mane and tail as he responded to Nick's signal and, once in his stride, the space between the two horses lengthened rapidly. Joanna did her best to spur the lesser animal to increased speed, but it wasn't in Sadie to deliver more than a faint quickness of pace. Soon Nick and Caliph were mere specks against the tree belt they were headed for.

Resigning herself to the steady jog, Joanna glanced round her at the rolling terrain, seeing the sun set behind distant mountains in multicoloured radiation. Nick had been right to leave the Ames place when they did. Soon it would be dark, making travel on horseback difficult until the moon rose sufficiently to light the treacherous hidden potholes and tree stumps.

Unfortunately, she was also left with the leisure to remember Alex's forbidding frown that morning when she had accepted with alacrity Nick's invitation to accompany him to Shirley's that day.

'Anna doesn't ride,' he stated, 'and I don't want to be responsible for broken legs or necks while she's my responsibility.'

His coldness had seeped through to her insides as he had known it would, she realised, her eyes meeting the forceful dominance in his.

Now, as she rounded the bend before the meeting place, she forced a smile to her lips when she saw Nick stretched on his back on the soft moss beneath a group of alders, Caliph close by snorting and pawing the inert figure with what she hoped was a gentle hoof.

'Come on, lazybones,' she called, dismounting from Sadie and throwing the reins over a handy bush. 'You can sleep all you want when we get home.'

The smile disappeared as she bent over Nick's prostrate form. It was too far-fetched that he should have fallen asleep so quickly and completely, and even before she had turned his averted head to disclose a seeping wound at his temple, she knew that his stillness was that of unconsciousness.

'Nick! Oh, Nick, please ...'

There was no response, and she looked wildly around. She had to get help—but where, in this isolated spot? Alex ... she must find Alex, he would know what to do. But he was at the Erikson place—was that closer than Clearwater? Would she be able to find it before darkness came?

With one last look at Nick, she rose from her knees and grasped Caliph's bridle. He would have to be the one to take her to Alex, Sadie would take for ever and a day. Without thinking further, she swung Caliph round and mounted even as the horse moved forward, accepting without question her light weight in the saddle more used to Alex's bulk. But Joanna was a familiar figure to him from the visits she had paid to the corrals with delectable titbits for his enjoyment.

As if sensing the urgency of their mission, the stallion stretched his legs to their utmost and Joanna crouched low over the saddle as the ground was swallowed up and left behind. Once headed in that direction, Caliph seemed to know the route to the Erikson place ... but how far was it?

Thankful now for Nick's suggestion that she wear casual clothes that day, she hugged the horse's sides with jeans-clad legs, and felt the breeze tear at her hair, tightly fastened into a ponytail.

Alternately begging and commanding the horse to greater speed, her thoughts spiralled between Nick lying helpless behind her and the hope that Caliph would not miss his footing again—which was the obvious explanation for the accident.

Light was fading rapidly when she saw at last signs of habitation whipping by them. Neat fenceposts enclosed square pastures, and the indistinct trail they had been following had turned into a well-trodden ranch roadway. The neatly painted Erikson house came looming up as Caliph instinctively passed the stockyards and stables. From the corner of her eye, Joanna saw a tall figure start up from a lawn chair, then freeze as he stared at horse and rider bearing down on him and the woman across the white patio table.

Automatically, expertly, Joanna brought Caliph to a snorting halt and half fell from the saddle into Alex's waiting arms.

'What in *hell*! ...' he exploded mightily, but his arms tightened protectively round her. Joanna wanted to rest her head against the cream knit shirt stretched over his muscular chest, to feel the heavy pound of his his heart against the erratic thud of her own ... but there was no time.

'Alex, you have to come,' she panted, stretching her neck to look earnestly up into his stunned face. 'It's Nick——'

'Didn't I tell you she was a little liar, Alex?' Paula's voice, strangely shrill, interrupted from behind. 'She couldn't have ridden Caliph like that if she——'

Alex turned his head and said fiercely: 'Shut up, Paula! Anna, what's happened to Nick?'

'He—Caliph must have stumbled and thrown him. He

hurt his head, but—I think he'll be all right if he gets—help right away.'

'Where did this happen?' Alex rapped, holding her away and staring fixedly into her eyes. 'Where is he?'

'About—five miles or so back along the trail, by a clump of trees, Sadie's tied up near him.' She shivered. 'I can show you where ... it's getting dark and you might not find him.'

'I'll find him,' he said grimly, 'without your help. There's something else I want you to do.' Turning to the tight-lipped Paula, he rapped out a series of instructions. 'Phone the doctor from here, then drive Anna home. Anna, you get things ready there. Nick can be put in my bed for the time being; see if you can find hot water bottles or something. Oh, Pete! ...'

Paula's brother had appeared round the corner of the house, listening attentively when Alex strode over and explained the situation to him. With a concerned glance at Joanna, he hurried back in the direction he had come from.

Joanna seemed frozen to the spot until Alex came back and looked narrowly down into her eyes. Paula had gone into the house to phone the doctor, but even without her acerbic presence, Joanna still felt uncomfortably aware that, by riding the mighty Caliph over that distance, she had blown her pretence of not knowing which end of a horse was up.

The swift indrawing of Alex's breath brought her eyes up to meet the astonished disbelief in his. 'My God ...' he said softly, nodding his head as if agreeing with his own thoughts, 'I should have known.'

'Kn-known what, Alex?'

He stared down at her for another moment or two, then seemed visibly to shake himself before saying roughly: 'Never mind now. We'll talk later.'

Swinging himself up on Caliph, he said no goodbyes as he rode off with Peter, who joined him on a mount only slightly less magnificent than Caliph.

Joanna had no time to ponder on the meaning of what he had said, yet it worried at the back of her mind all through the journey back to Clearwater, despite Paula's impudent probing into her reasons for concealing the fact that not only could she ride, but ride very well.

'I don't see why you hid it,' the fair girl said arrogantly, glancing sideways at Joanna's set profile. 'Unless you'd planned to catch Alex by playing dumb like you did that Saturday when he took you riding.'

'That's exactly why,' Joanna snapped, tired of the other girl's note of confident possession where Alex was concerned, although she had every right in the world to feel that way. 'I was out to snare Alex, and that seemed a cosy way to do it.'

Paula was unperturbed. 'Alex is the last man in the world you'll snare by telling him lies about yourself,' she said with a note of smugness. 'He hates people who are dishonest.'

'Then maybe he should be a little more honest himself in his personal relationships!' Joanna retorted waspishly, and immediately regretted the words when Paula turned her pale blue eyes on her.

'What do you mean by that? Surely you haven't taken his little flirtation with you seriously!' She chuckled bleakly when Joanna gasped and turned her head towards her. 'He told me all about it. You haven't been the first silly girl to lose her head over him, and probably you won't be the last. But he always comes back to me.'

Joanna leaned back weakly in her seat, and silence reigned for the rest of the short journey. At the house, she roused herself to enquire of the still seated Paula: 'Aren't you coming inside to help with Nick?'

'Certainly not. Illness of any kind upsets me, Alex understands that.'

Joanna turned blindly towards the steps as Paula swirled off down the drive. What was Alex letting himself in for with a wife like that? Around a ranch there were bound to be accidents of one kind or another. Illnesses too—if Alex was ill, would Paula turn her back on him in the same way?

Shaking herself out of the mood of self-pity rapidly overtaking her, Joanna went into action preparing Alex's bed to receive Nick. Had they found him yet? They must have by now, using the flashlights they had taken with them. Sadie would be a sizeable landmark.

At one moment the house was filled with waiting quiet, then all at once the hall was filled with noise as a deathly pale Nick, supported by Alex and Peter, was led towards the study. He was groggy, but at least he was conscious, Joanna thought as she hurried across to them. A white bandage circled his head, emphasising his pallor.

'Oh, Nick,' she breathed, 'I should have wrapped something round it, shouldn't I? I just didn't think.'

'Should have torn a few layers of your petticoats in ... best tradition,' he essayed with a grin, looking worse than ever.

'Is the doctor here?' Alex cut in brusquely.

Joanna shook her head, and he added: 'You'd better watch out for him while we get Nick into bed.'

'I've laid pyjamas out for him,' she said quietly, turning away from the scrutiny in his eyes.

Later, when the doctor had cleaned and re-dressed the wound and announced that Nick would be fit to meet his fate in two weeks, Joanna received instructions that she was to prepare only a clear soup for him, and then he would sleep the rest of the night.

Peter accepted the doctor's offer of a lift home, saying he would pick up his horse the next day. Her legs shaking in an unnatural way, Joanna carried the soup into the study on a tray. Alex was leaning negligently against the doorframe into the bedroom. His eyes took on a remote coolness as he stood aside for Joanna to pass him.

'Can you manage?' she asked the propped-up Nick, whose face was showing more colour despite the bandages.

'I could manage a lot more than this,' he eyed the soup balefully, then caught Joanna's hand as she straightened. 'Thanks for everything, Anna. I'd have been a goner if it hadn't been for you.'

'Hardly that,' Alex drawled. 'You were beginning to look around you when we found you.' He looked at Joanna. 'Have you called Shirley?'

Her face mirrored guilt at her forgetfulness. 'I'll do it now.'

'Don't bother, I will. And while I'm doing that,' he turned back to say, 'maybe you can rustle us up some food. I missed my dinner at the Eriksons'.'

'Give him some of this soup, Anna,' Nick offered wryly.

'I was thinking more along the lines of a thick, juicy steak with all the trimmings, including a fluffy baked potato,' Alex retorted with cruel relish, and Nick groaned.

Alex had his hand on the phone when Joanna asked stiffly if he had really meant that he wanted steak with all the trimmings.

'No,' he shrugged, 'a sandwich will do. One of your specials—Anna.'

Was it her imagination, or had he paused before saying her name? There was no way of telling from his face, because he had turned his back on her to use the telephone.

Her nerves were strung to taut wiriness by the time she returned to the study to collect his and Nick's dishes. The plate she had piled high with healthy-looking sandwiches and cherry tomatoes was empty, but there was no softening in his expression when he interpreted her look at the closed bedroom door.

'Nick's asleep,' he said from behind the desk. 'Leave those things for now, I want to talk to you. At least, I think it's time we had a talk, don't you, Anna? Or should I say—*Jo*-anna?' he asked, his voice deliberately quiet.

# CHAPTER TEN

For Joanna, it was as if he had roared from the bottom of the sea and sent reverberations ringing inside her head.

'Wh-what did you s-say?' she whispered, her eyes widening with shock and fastening on to his grim face. Without looking directly at his hand, she saw it lift something white from the desk.

'Know what this is, Miss Thomas?' He waved a thick, gold-embossed card before her eyes. Her heart sinking, she recognised her school crest—her school, and ... Liz's! It had never occurred to her that Alex would have saved such mementoes from his young sister's school-days.

'It's a programme for a gymkhana held at my sister's school on Vancouver Island six years ago. It was her last year there, so I saved this for her. As it happened, I was—substituting—for our parents that day, the first time I'd been to the school.' His brown fingers leafed through the thin inner pages of the programme. 'I remember being surprised at the standard of excellence, particularly in one girl a year or two younger than my sister. Yes, here it is. "Joanna Thomas. Joanna has been top of her year in equestrian pursuits since her arrival at the school four years ago. This year, she is reaching for the senior school's Triple Crown, and we wish her luck." As I recall,' Alex drawled, dropping the programme on the desk before him, 'Miss Thomas *was* successful—wasn't she?'

'How do I know?' she shrugged with a last-ditch show of negligence. 'There must be dozens of girls called Anna—or Joanna—Thomas. I told you, my father works in a factory. Is it likely he'd be able to send me to a fancy school like that?'

'It is if he happens to be the James Thomas who donated a—— what was it?' he leafed again through the programme, 'oh, yes—a new chemical lab to the school. That would be the multi-millionaire Thomas who *owns* several factories in Vancouver and elsewhere throughout the world.'

'C-Coincidence!'

'Coincidence be damned!' Alex slapped the flat of his hand on the desk with a resounding crack, startling her. 'I might forget a female face, a figure, a name—but I never, repeat *never*, forget how she looks on a horse,' he gritted, casting a regretful glance in the direction of the bedroom as if regretting the necessity of keeping his voice lowered. 'As soon as you appeared on Caliph, I knew I'd seen you on a horse somewhere. It didn't take me long to remember where.'

Joanna dropped with sudden weariness into the round-backed chair at one side of the desk. 'So what does it matter if my father's Thomas the millionaire or Thomas the plumber?'

His eyes registered amazement. 'Why in hell would a millionaire's daughter want to come down here and wash my socks and underwear?'

'Somebody has to wash them.'

'But why you?'

Joanna ran her fingers along the edge of the desk, not noticing the tightness that came to his mouth when he looked at the unkempt state of her nails.

'You wouldn't understand.'

'Try me.'

'Oh, I don't know. I just wanted to do something worthwhile, do it well. I'm not qualified in anything, and .. and when I met Liz that day in Vancouver, it seemed a wacky but exciting way to prove myself. I mean,' she spread her hands expressively, 'if I could make it here, I could make it anywhere. And I *have* made it here, Alex, haven't I?'

An odd expression flitted across his features as her eyes appealed to him. 'Yes, you've—made it here, An—Joanna.'

'You can call me Anna, it doesn't matter. I won't be here for much longer, will I?'

'That depends.' He took a cigar from his pocket and spent an inordinately long time in lighting it. Then he pushed back his chair and lifted his feet to a corner of the desk. 'Okay. Go ahead.'

She stared at him blankly. 'Go ahead with what?'

'Telling me about Joanna Thomas, the poor little rich girl.'

'It would take all night,' she laughed shortly, puzzled by his change of attitude. Reluctantly, the thought crept into her mind that the change had come about after his discovery of her identity. Was no man immune to her father's millions?

'I'm not doing anything for the rest of the night,' he puffed equally on his cigar. 'Go on, it'll be like therapy for you.'

And strangely, haltingly at first, she did tell him ... not just the facts, but the feelings the facts had provoked in her. The fierce missing of her mother, her father's pre-occupation with business, her forced interest in horses to the exclusion of everything else, the futile attempts at independence she had made, the disillusionment brought about by the knowledge that men saw her as her father's daughter rather than as herself.

She smiled tremulously as she finished and glanced at her watch. 'Your eyes are open, but I have an idea you're fast asleep behind them.'

'Far from it.' Alex swung his feet down from the desk where they had rested intermittently. The stubs of three cigars reposed in the ashtray at his elbow, the measure of brandy he had poured for himself less than half drunk. 'Do you realise you haven't stammered or stuttered once in all the time you've been telling me about you self?'

'And what does that mean, Professor?'

He pushed himself to his feet and came round to stand in front of her, a lazily mocking smile on his mouth as he reached down and pulled her up against him.

'It means, my dishonest darling, that you haven't lied to me once. As I've said before, you'd make a lousy actress apart from not being able to remember your lines. I can always tell when you're lying.'

'You can?' she breathed, too conscious all at once of his attraction for her, of his physical awareness of her as a woman.

'Of course. When you're telling the truth you look me right in the eye. When you're lying, you look anywhere but at my eyes. That's a valuable tool for a man to have with a woman,' he ended huskily, his mouth suddenly at her ear, sending fiery signals along her nerve ends.

'Alex, I—oh, Alex,' she breathed, reaching blindly for his mouth as it kissed lightly along her cheek. Obligingly, his lips covered hers and moved with such ardent sensuality there that Joanna's body arched naturally up to his.

Minutes later he dragged his mouth from hers and in a deeply husky tone: 'And what about this married man of yours? Is it really all over with him?'

Joanna's slim form trembled with laughter in his arms. 'I hope not!' she gurgled.

'What?'

'Stupid!' She lifted a hand to ruffle the crisp russet of his hair. 'The married man who was writing to me from Europe was Daddy ... only I couldn't let you know that, could I? An unemployed factory worker doesn't usually take vacations in Europe.'

Alex swore under his breath, his arms tightening to exert breathtaking pressure on her ribs. 'Do you know the hell you've put me through over that man? It was bad enough having Nick, Glen, Pete fall at your feet, but I couldn't stand the thought of a faceless man meaning more to you than I ever could.'

'Did you really care?' she asked, openly curious. 'You never show what you're feeling, so I—anyway, you won't suffer too much from my incompetence at the start,' she went off at a tangent, 'Daddy's sending replacements for your mother's crystal. I really am sorry I broke it, Alex.'

'It's not that important. It meant something to her because she went there and bought it on a happy vacation. And now,' he bent swiftly to scoop her light form into his arms, 'I'm going to go back to where we left off last night.'

So saying, he carried her to the broad sofa and lowered her on to it. Unfortunately, it was a reminder of Paula's telephone call the evening before, the one that had sent him hotfooting it over to the Erikson place that day.

The thought of Paula sent Joanna's hands to press up against his chest as he reached for her. 'Alex, please .:. don't ...'

He lifted himself from her, his eyes angrily puzzled.

'What do you mean, *don't*? Don't you like me to make love to you?'

'Of course I do,' she cried softly, 'it's just that I—that —oh, Alex,' she said despairingly, 'I don't sleep around.'

His head jerked up with such force that she felt sure his neck had almost snapped. 'You think that's what I want? A quick, cosy affair? What the hell kind of a man do you take me for? I want you for my *wife*, Anna! ...'

'Wife?' she repeated dazedly, eyes deepening to indigo as they searched the warm brown of his. 'But—Paula!'

Alex ran an impatient hand through his hair, doing nothing to prevent its spilling over on his forehead. 'Why do you keep bringing Paula into it? She hasn't meant anything to me in that way for years. We're friends, so we go out together now and then, but that's all there is between us now.'

'But the new house!' Joanna cried. 'You're building it for her ... you said so, everybody thinks so.'

Alex cast a watchful glance at the bedroom door, then bent his head closer to hers. 'The house was never intended for Paula and me. It's for Nick and Shirley. I wanted it to be a surprise wedding present for them, so I let them think I was having it built for my own use.'

'And Paula's,' Joanna added thoughtfully.

He shrugged. 'She was the only one available at the time. What matters is, do you think they'll like it?'

'They'll love it,' Joanna said dreamily, her fingers stroking absently through his hair.

'You're sure you prefer the old place?' he put anxiously. 'I could have swung from the rafters that day you came to the new house and said you liked it, but you prefer the old place.'

'I meant it.' She traced the outline of his mouth with

one finger, her brow wrinkling thoughtfully. 'Alex, when did you know that you—that you cared about me?'

He chuckled deep in his throat. 'When I felt a terrified little nose dive against my neck as I carried you across the creek the night you arrived. I think I knew then that I'd want to take care of you the rest of my life.'

'Oh, Alex, I think I knew it then, too ... although I was primed to fall in love with you long before that.'

'Oh?'

'Yes, when you came to school that time. I had a stupendous crush on you for weeks. I hadn't even seen you close up, but you had such a terrific physique!'

'*Had?*' he asked sternly.

'Have,' she corrected, running the flat of her palms up over his chest to the muscled hardness of his broad shoulders.

He bent his head swiftly and found her lips. Much later, when they stirred and reluctantly drew slightly apart, Alex said huskily: 'Do you think you can bear the idea of leaving the bright lights to marry a tough old rancher?'

'No, I don't think I could,' she frowned with mock seriousness, then smiled into his eyes. 'But I'll gladly leave all the bright lights in the world for the chance to be with the wonderful, handsome young rancher I love.'

'That should do to go on with,' Alex murmured contentedly against her lips.

**4 FREE Harlequin Romances**

### Get all the latest books before they're sold out!

As a Harlequin subscriber you actually receive your personal copies of the latest Romances immediately after they come off the press, so you're sure of getting all 6 each month.

### Cancel your subscription whenever you wish!

You don't have to buy any minimum number of books. Whenever you decide to stop your subscription just let us know and we'll cancel all further shipments.

**ur FREE
ft includes**

- *Anne Hampson* — Beyond the Sweet Waters
- *Anne Mather* — The Arrogant Duke
- *Violet Winspear* — Cap Flamingo
- *Nerina Hilliard* — Teachers Must Learn

# What readers say about Harlequin Romances

"I feel as if I am in a different world every time I read a Harlequin."

"Harlequins have been my passport to the world. I have been many places without ever leaving my doorstep."

"I like Harlequin books because they tell so much about other countries."

"Your books offer a world of knowledge about places and people."

# What the press says about Harlequin Romances...

"The most popular reading matter of American women today."
— *The Detroit News*

"Women have come to trust these stories about contemporary people, set in exciting foreign places."
— *Best Sellers*, New York

"Harlequin novels have a vast and loyal readership."
— *Toronto Star*